ABOUT

The daughter of a military father, Catherine Coles spent her childhood years devouring everything her school library had to offer.

Her favourite books were romance and mysteries. Her love for the Nancy Drew books led Catherine to check out every mystery story she could find. She soon found Agatha Christie, whose writing Catherine describes as 'brilliantly genius'.

Catherine writes cozy mysteries that take place in the English countryside. Her extremely popular Tommy & Evelyn Christie mysteries are set in 1920s North Yorkshire. Catherine lives in north east England with her two spoiled dogs who have no idea they are not human!

You can find Catherine online at www.catherinecoles.com.

If you would like to be amongst the first to know about her new releases, price drops, competitions, and special offers, please join Catherine's newsletter via her website.

### Books by Catherine Coles

*Murder at the Manor*
*Murder at the Village Fete*
*Murder in the Churchyard*
*Murder in Belgrave Square*
*Murder at the Wedding Chapel*
*Murder at Rochester Park*

# MURDER AT THE WEDDING CHAPEL

## A 1920S COZY MYSTERY

## CATHERINE COLES

INSPIRED PRESS LIMITED

EBook ISBN: 978-1-915126-03-0
Print ISBN: 978-1-915126-04-7

**Murder at the Wedding Chapel**

Editors: Sara Miller & Arnetta Jackson
Book design: Sally Clements

www.catherinecoles.com

❀ Created with Vellum

# CAST OF CHARACTERS

## Main Characters

Tommy Christie - The Seventh Earl of Northmoor, former police officer
Evelyn Christie - Policewoman during the Great War, Tommy's wife

## The Family

Lady Emily Christie - Tommy's great-aunt
Lady Victoria Bernard - Tommy's aunt
Elise Bernard - Lady Victoria's eldest daughter
Madeleine Bernard - Lady Victoria's younger daughter
Helen Christie - Tommy's mother
Constance Christie - Tommy's sister
Grace Christie - Tommy's sister
Henry (Harry) Christie - Tommy's brother

## The Guests

Andrew Parsons - The Marquess of York and Helen's fiancé
Lady Beatrice Dawson - The Marquess's eldest daughter
Leslie Dawson - Her husband
Lady Frances Lester - The Marquess's younger daughter
Nicholas Lester - Her husband
Sir Richard Carlisle - Helen's godfather
Frank Simmons - The Marquess's best man
Jane Simmons - His wife
Alexander Ryder - The Tenth Earl of Chesden
David Ryder - The Earl of Chesden's younger brother

Hugh Norton-Cavendish - Alexander & David's school friend

## The Staff

Wilfred Malton - The butler
Phyllis Chapman - The housekeeper
Mary O'Connell - The cook
Nora - The kitchen maid
Jack Partridge - The estate manager
Walter Davies - Tommy's valet
Frank Douglas - First footman
Arthur Brown - Second footman
Gladys Ferriby - Lady Emily's lady's maid
Doris - Evelyn's maid
Elsie Warren - Nanny/nursemaid

## The Villagers

John Capes - Vicar of the village church, St Augustus
Albert - The butcher's boy

## Others

Detective Inspector Andrews - Senior detective from York
Detective Sergeant Montgomery - Junior detective

# CHAPTER 1

*ugust 1922 - North Yorkshire*
"What terrible news about Hugh's father," Tommy said, looking over at his wife, Evelyn.

"Completely dreadful," she agreed. "Poor Hugh. Elise says he is quite devastated."

Hugh was engaged to Tommy's cousin, Elise Bernard, and earlier that day had received a telegram to say his father had died in a shooting incident. "He suggested his father's death may not have been as accidental as the police are trying to make out."

Evelyn turned to him and smiled. "Oh, Tommy. You must not see murder in every death."

"It wasn't me," Tommy protested. "Hugh thinks there may be some sort of misadventure on his father's part."

"Goodness," Evelyn lowered her voice as though someone may overhear them, which was very doubtful given they were talking in their bedroom. "Are you telling me Hugh thinks his father killed himself?"

Tommy grimaced. "Unfortunately, I am. Hugh thinks the monstrous debts his father has incurred may have finally become too much for him."

Evelyn shook her head. "How selfish. All that means for Hugh is that he has inherited those debts. Then there will be death duties to consider. Oh, that poor man."

He knew his wife referred to Hugh, rather than to his father. "Rochester Park has been neglected for centuries."

Tommy had concentrated on ways to make their home, Hessleham Hall, profitable when he inherited the estate and his title: the Earl of Northmoor. Although he had a very good estate manager, he worked countless hours to ensure the security of both the house and the accompanying land.

"Elise tells me some rooms are quite inhabitable."

Tommy moved over to stand behind Evelyn, who was sitting at the dressing table applying fresh make-up.

"It would be best for Hugh to sell the estate, pay off everything that is owed, then start again somewhere smaller."

"Do you think he will sell Rochester Park? Would you have sold Hessleham Hall if you were in his position?" She turned around to face him, a worried frown creasing her forehead.

"Rochester Park is his home, and it's been in his family for centuries. I think he'll try everything before admitting defeat. And you know, selling this old place." Tommy spread his hands wide. "Was never in my thoughts. It's my duty to run Hessleham Hall and leave it, intact, for the next generation."

"Whoever that may be." Evelyn turned back to look in the mirror.

Tommy dropped to one knee beside her and moved the stool around so he could look into her face. "If it isn't our son, it'll likely be a nephew."

"I know," she whispered. "I count my blessings every single day. Truly I do, Tommy. This house and our family give me so much joy."

"I can remember a time not so long ago when you detested this house."

She smiled. "That was before it became ours. Now it feels special, as do the people who live and work here."

"When you love something, it's easy to overlook its faults."

She leaned forward and pressed her lips against his. "Which is why I adore you so very much."

That wasn't quite what he meant, but he couldn't help but grin at his wife's playful retort. "And I am very grateful, darling, that you love me despite my obvious flaws."

She smiled. "You are a very lucky man."

When he inherited their home just over a year before, the only other family member that lived with them was Great-Aunt Em. Now Aunt Victoria and her daughters, Elise and Madeleine, lived with them along with Madeleine's baby, Josephine.

"I know how much you love having the girls and Josephine here every day." He reached out and cupped Evelyn's face with one hand.

She didn't need to speak the words in her heart, because he could see them in her pain-filled eyes. They were incredibly fortunate with their home and family, but the one thing they both wanted more than anything else had so far eluded them—a baby of their own.

"Elsie has been wonderful. I'm so glad she could join us." Elsie Warren, a young woman from the village, now worked as nursemaid to the family. "We need all the help we can get this weekend."

It was Friday night, and the next morning his mother Helen was to marry her fiancé, Andrew Parsons, Marquess of York. "The last time the house was this busy was when Uncle Charles was killed last summer."

"Tommy!" Evelyn exclaimed. "What a thing to say! You will jinx your mother's wedding."

"I do wish something would happen to stop it." His words were said in haste, but he did not wish he hadn't said them. If he couldn't be honest with Evelyn, who could he tell his darkest worries and deepest fears to?

"You don't like Andrew, do you?"

Tommy ran a hand through his hair. "Not one bit. I don't really have a quantifiable reason, either. There's just something about him that makes the hairs on the back of my neck stand on end."

"We've learned to listen to our instincts, haven't we?"

Over the last year, they had been involved in four different mysteries—all of which they had solved. "We have, but on this occasion, I can't rely on my intuition to convince my mother that marrying Andrew would be a monumental mistake."

"You don't think she would listen to you? Darling, have you tried?"

"I tried very carefully," he said. "As soon as I broached the subject, she closed me down straightaway. She was nice about it, didn't take offence, but said she thinks I'm jealous and I'd feel this way about any man taking my father's place."

"Are you sure that isn't what this is? He seems exceptionally charming to me."

"He is charming." Tommy smiled. "That's part of the problem."

"The man marrying your mother shouldn't be charming?" Evelyn enquired, lifting an eyebrow. "You would have something to say if her fiancé were not solicitous."

"I can't put my finger on it," Tommy said. "There's something about him that is decidedly false."

"Have you spoken to Aunt Em?" Evelyn asked. "She is very good at reading people, and you can trust she would certainly tell you exactly what she thinks."

"The only problem is what would I do if her opinion is the same as mine? Her thoughts will not hold sway with my mother. Father was Aunt Em's favourite nephew. Mother will simply think Em is as biased against Andrew as I am."

A knock sounded on the door, and Evelyn's maid, Doris, came into the room. "You asked me to remind you of the time, My Lady."

"Of course. Thank you, Doris."

Tommy looked at his watch. "You're going down now? Isn't it rather early?"

"It may be early for someone who doesn't care much about her guests," Evelyn retorted. "I want to check everything is alright in the kitchen given the extra work, speak to Mrs Chapman to be certain our guests are all happy, and finally, I want to pop to the nursery to say goodnight to Josephine before Elsie puts her to bed."

"Goodness." Tommy shared a grin with Doris. "Will you have time to do all of that before dinner?"

"I most certainly will." Evelyn took one last look in the mirror and then got to her feet. "Will you have time to get ready for company?"

Tommy shrugged and looked down from his dinner suit to his impeccably shined shoes. "I've been ready for ages."

Evelyn pointed at his face with her forefinger and then touched it to the corner of his mouth. "I think your face could do with a bit of a scrub."

Doris hid a smile behind her hand as her mistress went sailing out of the room. Without looking in Evelyn's mirror, Tommy knew his lips held a trace of his wife's bright red lipstick from the affectionate kiss she'd given him.

He went through the adjoining door to his own room and into the small bathroom. Removing the makeup from his face was a small price to pay for his wife's favour and one he'd be willing to pay for the rest of his life.

No one needed to tell him how lucky he was to have such a loving wife. He wondered if Andrew Parsons valued his wife-to-be as much.

~

*E*velyn slipped down the back stairs after saying goodnight to Josephine and went into the drawing room. She was satisfied there was nothing more she could do that night to make their guests more comfortable.

Their cook, Mrs O'Connell, was already well ahead with the preparations for the food for the wedding the next day. She could relax.

"Gin and tonic, My Lady?" Malton, the butler, asked as she entered the room.

"Make it a double, please, it's been a busy day."

He nodded, and Evelyn took a seat on the sofa next to Aunt Em. "Good evening, Lord York."

"Lady Northmoor." Andrew Parsons raised his glass slightly to Evelyn by way of greeting. "Surprised your husband allows you to drink excessively before dinner. Surely there's enough wine served during an evening meal for a lady's delicate constitution?"

His overbearing assumption threw Evelyn, but Aunt Em was, as usual, not lost for words. "I always think that rather depends on one's dinner companions."

"Indeed." He turned to Malton. "I think I shall have another."

"Of course, Lord York." Malton immediately served the man another drink. Evelyn had instructed the staff that whatever Helen's fiancé wanted, he got, without hesitation. She had worked very hard on her relationship with her mother-in-law, but still found her frosty and rather prickly for a friendship to blossom.

It still made no sense to her that Helen had asked her and Tommy to host her wedding. Lord York had a suitable estate of his own, and it seemed rather odd to her he would want to get married at the family home of his wife's deceased husband.

The drawing room filled with close family members who

were to attend the wedding the next morning. Evelyn was glad when Lord York turned to talk to one of his daughters, but his loud voice carried across the room.

"Beatrice, what is that garment you're wearing? I do hope you have something more sensible and suitable for my wedding tomorrow. What will people think?"

Beatrice, the Marquess's eldest daughter, flushed nearly as pink as her gown. Full of frills and flounces, it wasn't the type of dress Evelyn favoured and, unfortunately, it only highlighted Beatrice's full figure.

"I'm sorry, Father."

"Dawson?" Lord York rounded on Beatrice's husband. "What do you have to say for yourself, man?"

"Lord York?" Leslie Dawson shook his head, confusion clearly etched on his pasty face. It was a mystery to most people that Andrew Parsons had allowed his eldest child to marry a man with no title. However, Tommy told Evelyn it was probably because the Dawson family was amongst the richest in the north of England. Sensibly, the Marquess had ensured that his family's estate would be financially secure for the next generation.

"I presume you saw your wife before she came down for dinner?" Lord York looked derisively at his daughter. "She looks like a blancmange."

"What an awful man," Aunt Em whispered. "I almost feel sorry for Helen."

"Why almost?"

"She's always been the most dreadful snob," Aunt Em went on. "I imagine the thought of being a Marchioness gives her an immunity to her fiancé's dreadful behaviour."

"He's rather vulgar," Evelyn agreed. "Tommy said upstairs he did not like Lord York, but I must admit I've found him rather amiable until now."

"Perhaps he no longer feels as though he needs to be on his best behaviour?" Aunt Em suggested. She nudged Evelyn.

"Here comes Helen. Let's see what he has to say about her attire, because I'm sure he'll have an opinion."

"Darling!" Lord York exclaimed effusively and bent theatrically as he lifted one of Helen's gloved hands to his lips. He air kissed and then smiled indulgently. "You look absolutely divine."

"In this old thing?" Helen giggled coquettishly.

"It's so new, I can practically see the stitch marks from the seamstress's needle." Aunt Em took a sip of her drink.

Beatrice's face changed from pure embarrassment to loathing as she watched her father fawn over her stepmother-to-be.

"Thank you, Malton." Evelyn accepted her drink from the butler, then turned back to Aunt Em. "Beatrice looks positively murderous."

"My dear Evelyn." Aunt Em pinned Evelyn with one of her infamous looks. "Have you learned nothing in the last year? We should banish that word from the vocabulary of the Christie family."

"We could certainly try," Evelyn agreed. "But I don't think it would change a thing. Some people are obviously born with a certain predilection toward the darker side of life."

"Unfortunately, too many of them practice their evil around my family." Aunt Em put her empty glass on the side table next to her. "That worries me a great deal."

Evelyn reached out to pat Aunt Em's arm. It was very rare that the old lady showed anything but a brusque exterior and a general dislike for people who were not as forthright as herself. "I know you worry about us, but we're all very sensible about keeping our eyes peeled for trouble."

"I'm afraid I disagree." Aunt Em pursed her lips thoughtfully. "When murder is afoot, you and Tommy involve yourselves immediately. That doesn't strike me as sensible at all."

"I'm not sure we could have done anything any differently." Evelyn leaned a little closer to Aunt Em to ensure none of the guests overheard her words. "Every murder we have investigated has implicated one of our friends or family. Don't you remember Tommy was arrested for Uncle Charles's murder?"

"That was quite ridiculous," Aunt Em agreed. "Though I was convinced Charles's equally awful son, Eddie, had done away with his father."

"Strange to think if that hadn't happened, we wouldn't be here now," Evelyn mused. "How different our lives would be."

"You two have breathed life and love into this old house," Aunt Em said. "Although the way it came about may be less than ideal, especially for poor Charles and Eddie, I'm glad you and Tommy are here."

Evelyn was very fond of Em. She could scarcely believe how in awe of her she had been when she first met Tommy's family. Now she was a very dear friend, a staunch ally, and the woman Evelyn admired most in the world.

"You do know you're my very favourite aunt?"

"I am not your aunt, and neither is this the time or place for overly dramatic sentiments," Em replied with a slight smile that belied her dismissive words.

Evelyn smiled in response. "I am well aware, Aunt Em, that despite what you may say, you love me just as dearly as I love you."

"Goodness." Aunt Em blinked. "Just how much gin did Malton put into your glass?"

~

Tommy tried to calculate how much longer he had to be polite to his mother's fiancé before he could excuse himself. Sadly, the answer was an interminable length of time. He was the host. It would be considered poor form for him to leave any time soon.

He'd sat through dinner, then smoking with the other gentleman, before joining the ladies in the drawing room. There wasn't anything specific the Marquess of York had done wrong. He was polite in conversation, seemed interested when speaking to Tommy about Hessleham Hall and the estate, and his behaviour toward Helen was exactly what every son would want for their mother. Yet there was something he couldn't put his finger on about the man.

He watched as the Marquess moved toward his youngest daughter. Tommy edged closer and caught the end of the Marquess's words. "...your hair like that on purpose? I find that extremely hard to believe, Frances."

Frances Lester raised a hand to her hair. "You don't like it, Father? I thought it rather becoming."

Andrew Parsons gave a sarcastic chuckle. "Neither of you girls should try thinking. You're just like your mother. She wasn't a brilliant thinker either. Not at all like my Helen. Just look at her. Grace, poise, and she's kept a jolly decent figure despite her age."

"I'd rather you didn't speak about my mother like that, especially in front of company." Tommy kept his voice low, but firm.

"I'm sure I didn't mean any disrespect." He glared at Tommy.

"What are my favourite men talking about?" Helen glided to Andrew's side and placed a hand on his arm.

"I was praising your virtues, my dear, but it seems your son is a little offended by my effusiveness."

"Really, Thomas?" His mother looked at him with such pleading in her eyes that Tommy broke into a wide smile.

"I'm certain it was a simple misunderstanding."

"It most certainly was not." Andrew stared at Tommy, his dark eyes glittering with malice. There was no evidence of his infamous charm on show now. Tommy hadn't trusted the man, but he hadn't expected this level of hostility either. "I praised your mother, and you were rude to me."

"Perhaps we should just…" Helen began.

Andrew put his hand on top of Helen's and removed it from his arm. Tommy looked down to see the other man gripping his mother's hand tightly in his. She looked shocked, nervous, and more than a little afraid. "I will handle this, dear."

"Please let go of my mother's hand." Tommy struggled to keep his temper under control. The Marquess was nothing but a bully.

"Helen, do you want me to let go of your hand?"

His mother gave a tight little smile. "Of course not, my darling."

Andrew gave Helen an adoring smile and, for a moment, Tommy wondered if he'd got it all wrong. But he looked back at his mother's hand, still held tightly in Andrew's grasp, and knew he hadn't.

There was nothing he could do here in the drawing room, surrounded by their family and friends, but he couldn't just stay out of it and leave things the way they were. Not when his mother was due to marry the man the very next day. "Perhaps we could talk about this somewhere private?"

"Nothing to discuss, old man," Andrew replied affably. "You were mistaken. I rather think you can apologise here. No need to do that privately."

"I will not apologise for asking you to speak respectfully about my mother."

Andrew turned to Frances. "Is Lord Northmoor mistaken? Did I say anything that could be construed as disrespectful about Helen?"

"You were very complimentary about Mrs Christie," Frances said dutifully.

"See?" Andrew said triumphantly. "It appears that the only person with an issue here is you."

"Mother…"

"Thomas, please," Helen said. "You're embarrassing me in front of my new family."

Evelyn moved next to him, and Tommy forced himself to relax. "Is everything alright, my love?"

"Of course." Tommy looked at his mother once more. "Mother was just letting me know how much she is looking forward to spending more time with her new family."

Helen flinched at the barb, as Tommy knew she would. She had never been the most attentive of mothers, but since the death of his father, she had been even more detached. Was this what she was like with his siblings? How had Constance, Grace, and Harry coped with the death of their father and their mother's withdrawal into herself? Tommy hated that he hadn't realised before now how difficult things must have been for his sisters and brother. Young Harry was barely nineteen.

Why hadn't he thought before now, to check what arrangements were in place for them after the wedding? "Mother, what is happening to your house after your wedding?"

"Andrew thinks it best if we sell the house. It seems silly to keep two houses when we won't need the one in the village."

"What about Grace, Constance, and Harry? What is to become of them?"

"They're adults," Andrew stated blandly. "It is time they make their own way in the world. Your mother can't afford to coddle them forever."

Tommy stared at his mother, waiting for her to disagree with Andrew, but she said nothing. Small creases around her mouth told him she was struggling with the conversation, but she would not contradict Andrew's words.

Was that because she approved of his words, or because

she dared not speak her mind? Was she frightened of her fiancé?

"Now dear," Andrew said conversationally. "Why don't you run along and have that discussion with Thomas you mentioned to me earlier? It's a little late in the day, but better late than never."

The way his mother looked at Andrew reminded Tommy of a child who was beseeching his parent not to make him do something he didn't want to do. "Perhaps now is not the best time?"

"Now is the perfect time." Andrew squeezed Helen's hand. "Off you go, dear."

Tommy waited until his mother was sitting in one of the high-backed leather chairs in the billiard room before he spoke. "Are you going ahead with the wedding tomorrow?"

"Of course." His mother raised her chin as she met his gaze. "What a ridiculous question, Thomas."

He picked up her left hand, the one her fiancé had held firmly with his own. Tommy frowned as he looked at the deep indentations on the fingers on either side of her ostentatious engagement ring. The expensive jewellery reminded him he had known nothing of his mother's relationship with Andrew Parsons until she wrote to him asking if he and Evelyn would host their wedding.

"Does he often hurt you like this?"

"He was simply holding my hand," Helen replied. "Perhaps a little too firmly, but he didn't hurt me. Please don't make such a fuss."

Tommy fought to find the right words. The ones he wanted to say: Call it off, I don't like him were not enough. "I didn't like his behaviour this evening."

"You embarrassed him, and he's already so very nervous about the wedding tomorrow."

He couldn't argue the point, and he would not make things worse by defending his words to Andrew. In his view, it wasn't acceptable for Andrew to refer to his mother's body shape in polite society—especially when he was doing so to insult his children.

Tommy held in the deep sigh that wanted to escape his lips—how could a son advise his mother on her relationship when it was clear her mind was made up? "What did you want to talk to me about?"

Helen shifted uncomfortably in her seat and opened the evening bag on her lap. "Can I smoke in here?"

"You smoke?"

She laughed. If she aimed for gay and indifferent, she missed her mark. The sound was forced. "Darling, everyone smokes these days."

His mother didn't. Tommy stopped short of saying his father would never have allowed it. Did that make his father any better than Andrew, who seemed to be in complete control of Helen and her actions and choices. He had never heard his father speak harshly to his mother and he certainly wouldn't have spoken to her as Andrew had that evening. When Andrew suggested Helen speak to Tommy, it was as though he was giving instructions to a small child—it was clear he expected complete obedience.

He got to his feet and brought an ashtray over and placed it on the mahogany occasional table next to Helen. "Mother?"

She placed a thin black cigarette into a holder and lit it. Looking at him through the smoke, she swallowed deeply. "This is rather awkward."

Suddenly, it was blindingly obvious to Tommy what his mother wanted to talk to him about. Andrew said she was to sell her house. Grace, Constance, and Harry were to live independently. Hadn't Andrew said they were old enough to support themselves?

Andrew had sent her to ask him for money!

He decided not to prolong the difficult conversation. "How much do you need?"

Helen inhaled deeply, then blew out a stream of smoke. "It's not really about the amount. You do see I can't really go to Andrew empty handed, don't you?"

"I see he has sent you to do a man's job." Tommy wished he'd brought his after dinner brandy into the room with him. "If there was a question of some sort of dowry required, he should have spoken to me man to man."

"You were in London when we became engaged," Helen said sulkily.

"We were in London in April, Mother. It is now August. He's had plenty of time to approach me."

"Does that mean you're not willing to part with some of your Christie money to help your own mother?"

She wouldn't be asking him if he hadn't inherited the house and estate from the family. But then, would Andrew be marrying his mother if he wasn't the Earl of Northmoor? If he were still plain Thomas Christie, former police detective, and latterly captain in the British army? From what he knew about Andrew Parsons, the answer to that was no.

He had heard no rumours that the Marquess of York had financial problems, but that didn't mean it wasn't the reason Andrew wanted money from his fiancée's wealthy son. Or, perhaps, the man was simply greedy.

"I didn't say that."

"Thank you, darling, I knew you wouldn't let me down." The tension in her shoulders relaxed and warmth flooded into her eyes. "My dear eldest son."

"How much money are we talking about?"

Helen named a sum that made Tommy's need for brandy immediate. He walked over to the drink cabinet in the corner of the room and poured himself a large measure. Drinking half of it in one swallow, he walked back over to his seat.

"Darling?"

"I need to think about it," he said at last. "It's such a large sum. I don't feel comfortable giving you an answer tonight."

"Of course, darling, I completely understand."

There was one more question he needed to ask before he let his mother off the hook completely. "What is to happen to Constance, Grace, and Harry?"

"Andrew wishes to marry me. Obviously he accepts I have children, but he expects them to be independent, as his children are."

"His children are much older than yours and have children of their own. Harry is barely nineteen."

Regret flashed in his mother's eyes before she looked away and stubbed out her cigarette. "You will look after them, won't you, darling? After all, you have this enormous house. You have been so very fortunate."

"I will need to speak to Evelyn." Tommy got to his feet. "We should get back to the others."

"Yes, of course. Thank you, darling." She fastened her bag and offered her cheek to Tommy.

For the first time in his life, he was reluctant to kiss his mother's cheek.

# CHAPTER 2

*E*velyn held on tightly to Davey's lead. He was still as headstrong as he had been as a puppy. Even the younger Mary trotted happily next to Evelyn whilst her mother, Nancy, galloped on ahead across the lawn.

She'd be glad when this wedding was over, and things could get back to normal. Tommy had been tense and worried after his discussion with his mother the previous evening, and Evelyn could understand why. What sort of mother put her own needs above those of her children? One like her own, Evelyn supposed, but she hadn't thought Tommy's would ever be so selfish. Evelyn's own mother had spent more time caring for her dogs than she had Evelyn or her sister, Millicent.

Taking Tommy's siblings into their home wasn't a problem. She enjoyed the company of his sisters very much. Though she perhaps needed to talk to her husband about a few issues. Harry had consumed decidedly too much wine at dinner and not appeared in the drawing room afterward. Then there was the issue of Constance and Alexander Ryder.

She and Tommy had first met Alexander Ryder, now the 10th Earl of Chesden, at their home in Belgrave Square earlier that year. He had not made a favourable impression on either of them but had seemed very taken with the elder Christie sister in the drawing room the previous night. Evelyn didn't want to add to Tommy's worries, but he would be cross if he wasn't aware of the burgeoning friendship.

Alexander Ryder wasn't a family friend, but his younger brother, David, was engaged to Tommy's cousin Madeleine. After the ignominy of his father's death, social invitations for Alexander had dried up and David had begged Tommy to invite his brother to the wedding so Alex could escape from the London gossip.

Evelyn's mind turned to nicer thoughts. Her best friend, Isolde, was due to give birth any day now, and each time she heard the shrill trill of the telephone, she hoped it might be news from Isolde's husband, village doctor Teddy Mainwaring about the arrival of their baby.

She consoled herself with the fact she only had the rest of the day to get through, then guests would start leaving the next day and their lives would return to what passes for normality again around the estate. Though what that would mean for Helen, she didn't know. It had upset Tommy terribly when telling her about the discussion he had with his mother the previous evening, and how he was certain Andrew Parsons would not make a good husband.

Certainly, from what she had seen, the Marquess's behaviour toward Beatrice was less than acceptable. Wedding nerves were no excuse for being cruel to one's own child. Although he had seemed perfectly kind to Helen before dinner, Tommy's report of his behaviour afterwards meant he had serious concerns about Helen's safety with her new husband.

Evelyn hadn't intended to walk toward the small wedding chapel on the grounds of Hessleham Hall, but as she rounded the corner of the house and the pretty brick building came into view, she couldn't resist taking a peek inside.

In a few scant hours, the florist from the village would finish arranging flowers on the ends of the wooden pews, the vicar John Capes would stand at the front with Andrew Parsons and his best man, Frank Simmons. Helen would be at the entrance to the chapel on Sir Richard's arm, waiting to be given away to her new husband.

As they approached, Nancy paused at the low brick wall around the chapel and threw back her head and howled. The hair on the back of Evelyn's neck prickled, and a sense of foreboding raced down her spine.

There was only one other time Nancy had acted in such a peculiar way. That particular morning was etched in Evelyn's mind. On the morning of the village fete, held on the grounds of Hessleham Hall, she and Tommy had found the body of the local member of parliament dead in the stream. It wasn't possible for history to repeat itself, was it?

She asked herself that as she forced herself to move closer to Nancy. Davey stopped pulling on his lead and looked up at her as though begging her not to move closer to whatever was distressing Nancy.

Evelyn patted Nancy's head. "It's alright, old girl."

She peered over the wall, not wanting to see what was on the other side, but needing to put her mind at rest. To her great relief, there was nothing there.

Fastening Davey and Mary's leads to the iron gate in the centre of the wall, she walked down the path to the heavy wooden door of the chapel.

Evelyn took a deep breath and put her hand on the door. They never locked the chapel, but the latch ensured the door stayed closed. However, it slowly creaked open under the slight pressure from her palm.

Nancy howled louder.

Forcing herself to breathe normally, Evelyn stepped into the chapel. At once, she could see a pair of shoes on the stone floor as though someone had lain down to sleep. Of course!

Evelyn berated herself for being so dramatic. Harry must have stumbled around outside the previous night and ended up sleeping off his overindulgence in the chapel.

She moved forward quickly, keen to wake him and get him back to the house so he could start getting ready for his mother's wedding.

Only as she got closer, she realised two things at the same time. The man on the ground had streaks of silver in his dark hair, and he certainly wasn't sleeping.

Andrew Parsons lay face up on the flagstones with a knife sticking out of his stomach. His hands rested on the hilt of the weapon as though he intended to remove it but lacked the strength.

Evelyn sagged onto the front pew and braced her hands on her knees. She let her head fall forward as she struggled to get herself under control. Her hands shook, and she took one more look at the body to be certain of exactly what she had seen.

Not surprisingly, everything was exactly as it was the first time she looked. The Marquess of York was still dead.

~

"How is darling Helen taking it?" Sir Richard Carlisle asked Tommy as they sat together in the billiard room.

"She doesn't know yet." Tommy grimaced. "Her maid said she took a sleeping draught last night, so she hasn't woken yet. As soon as she's awake, I shall let her know."

"I don't envy you, my boy, she was devoted to the Marquess."

"Was she?" Tommy asked in surprise.

"Well, yes, of course." Sir Richard raised an eyebrow. "Why would you think differently?"

"I didn't know the Marquess very well. I only met him a

handful of times before he arrived yesterday for the wedding but I got the impression he was a rather dour man and not particularly kind to his family, or my mother."

"If I may speak plainly, Tommy?"

"Of course, Sir Richard. Please do."

Sir Richard Carlisle was Helen's godfather and so was a man Tommy had known his entire life. As a young boy, Tommy had referred to him as 'Uncle Richard', as children often did toward good friends of their parents.

"Your mother was never the type of woman who could function for long without a strong man in her life. I'm surprised it has taken her this long to consider getting married again."

"My father has only been gone…"

"Tommy, forgive me for my bluntness, but your father has been dead for over three years. Your mother is still in her fifties. You see the Marquess as a severe type of fellow, but lots of women of your mother's generation like a powerful man who tells them what to do. It makes them feel secure."

Tommy couldn't imagine what Evelyn would do if he started telling her how to dress, or how to act, or who she could and couldn't have as friends. Well, that wasn't strictly true. He knew well that Evelyn would tell him to drop his attitude or find a new wife. Their marriage was very much based on mutual respect and with both partners being equal.

"I say, do you know who the heir presumptive is?" Tommy asked, steering the conversation away from his mother. It made him feel rather queer discussing her personal life.

"Absolutely no idea. Obviously, the girls cannot inherit the title. I seem to remember there's a cousin in India." Sir Richard eyed Tommy suspiciously. "Are you thinking someone bumped him off for his title?"

He'd rather believe that than think his mother had something to do with the Marquess's death. Though she hadn't seemed overtly worried about her fiancé's behaviour when he'd spoken to her the previous evening. Of course, if Helen had wanted him dead, it would've made more sense for her to kill him after the wedding when she was his next of kin.

Tommy shrugged. "It's possible, isn't it? The war affected the lineage of so many families, York could've had a third cousin here for the wedding and not even be aware of it himself."

Sir Richard brushed the ends of his luxurious silver-hued moustache. "It would have made more sense for the fellow to have married a woman young enough to give him more children. I never understand men who don't secure the future of their families by prioritising an heir."

Tommy smothered an impolite laugh before it leapt out of his mouth. "You don't have children!"

"That is precisely why I can be so wise about the subject. I was so busy with my career, I left getting married until it was too late. No young thing of childbearing age wanted to marry an old buffer like me, so I remained single. Not like you, my boy, married nice and early."

Tommy recalled the advice given to him by his good friend, Teddy Mainwaring, sometimes conceiving a child took longer for some couples than for others. It was cold comfort given the doctor's wife had walked down the aisle already carrying their first child and he'd been married to Evelyn now for over six years—despite many of those being while he was serving during the war.

"Do you ever regret giving such focus to your career that you didn't marry?"

Sir Richard puffed out his chest. "I served my country with honour and distinction. Some things are more important than passing on a family name."

"Of course, I understand that. I hope you didn't find my question too impertinent."

"Thomas Christie." Sir Richard looked at Tommy with

clear affection in his blue eyes. "I've known you since you were a babe in arms. If you cannot ask me questions without me taking offence, who can?"

Evelyn knocked on the door to announce her presence. "Darling? Your mother is awake."

Tommy looked at Sir Richard and reluctance flooded through him. "I should get it over with."

Sir Richard put a comforting hand on Tommy's shoulder. "If you don't feel up to it, I'll do it."

"I couldn't ask that of you." Tommy grasped Sir Richard's hand in a firm shake. "But thank you for offering. You're a true gentleman."

Dread made his footsteps heavy as he walked across the room to join Evelyn.

~

Tommy knocked on the door to his mother's room and waited for her maid to open the door. When she did, her white face showed how keen she was to escape before her mistress found out what had happened to her fiancé earlier that morning.

Evelyn paused outside the room, but Tommy beckoned her to follow him.

Helen was sitting up in bed. She pulled her wrap tighter around her shoulders on seeing her visitors. Tommy sat awkwardly on the side of the bed. "I'm desperately sorry to be the bearer of bad news, Mother."

"Bad news?" Helen asked, then inexplicably patted her hair as though she wanted to look her best for the news that was to come.

"It's the Marquess…that is, Andrew…your intended."

"What about him?" Helen shot a glance toward the window. "Has he left?"

She covered her face with her hands and sobbed. Tommy

steeled himself against his mother's emotions. "Mother, I need you to listen to me."

Helen dropped her hands and looked at Tommy with suspicion in her tear-filled eyes. Then she turned her gaze on Evelyn. "He hasn't run out on the wedding, yet you are both in my bedroom before I'm even dressed."

Evelyn wanted to point out that it was after nine, but she was aware many ladies didn't rise until much later. She couldn't abide lying in bed for half the morning, not when she could be up and walking her dogs in the fresh country air.

"I'm afraid there's been an incident..."

"Incident?" Helen interrupted. "What do you mean, an incident?"

"Evelyn found Andrew this morning inside the chapel."

"And?" Helen made a 'move it along' motion with her hand. "Thomas, I have never known you to use so many words when two or three would probably do nicely."

"He's dead."

Evelyn glared at her husband. There was circumventing the truth, then there was baldly stating it with no attempt to soften the blow. Tommy jumped right to the latter.

"No!" Helen shrieked. "That cannot be right."

She scrambled to get out of bed, then her hands grasped the front of Tommy's shirt. He grabbed her hands and tried to pull her into an embrace. "I'm desperately sorry."

Helen slapped his hands away, untangled herself from her sheets, and got to her feet. "I must go to him."

"The village policeman is with him. I have telephoned to York, and they will send detectives over as soon as they can."

"You've got it wrong!" Helen wailed. "He can't be dead."

"I'm afraid I discovered the body," Evelyn said calmly. "There is no mistake."

"But we're marrying today." The enormity of the revelation seemed to hit Helen all at once and she sank into the chair next to the fireplace. "What shall I do?"

"There's nothing anyone can do at the moment." Evelyn moved over to sit opposite her mother-in-law. "Tommy, why don't you find Mrs Chapman and ask her to send tea up to your mother's room?"

"Yes, of course." Relief relaxed the worry lines on his face, and he looked at her gratefully. "You'll call if you need me?"

Evelyn nodded, and Tommy quickly left the room. "Dr Mainwaring has already been round and confirmed the sad news."

"Why did no one wake me before now?"

"I understand your maid tried, but she was aware you had taken a sleeping draught last night and she said she could not rouse you."

"I insist the girl is dismissed immediately. She couldn't have tried hard to wake me. I should have been with him."

"When did you last see him?" Evelyn asked cautiously.

"Before I went to speak to Tommy." A flush started in Helen's cheeks and flowed down to her neck. "I suppose he told you what we discussed?"

"He did."

Helen covered her face again. "I won't need that money now, will I? Oh, I'm so mortified I had to ask my own son for money."

"Was the Marquess really in such financial difficulty?"

Helen looked horrified. "Of course not. He said it was only right I came into the marriage with money. If I was a young girl getting married, no one would ask these questions or thinking it in the least bit strange."

Evelyn didn't think it was worth pointing out that Helen wasn't a first-time bride with a dowry provided by her father. She was a middle-aged woman getting married for the second time to a seemingly rich peer, but asked for a sizeable sum of money from her son.

"The police will, of course, wish to speak to you when they arrive."

"Me?" Helen squeaked, jabbing a finger into her chest.

"I'm afraid so," Evelyn confirmed. "You were his fiancée and so they will want to know everything you can tell them about him. Whether he had enemies, that sort of thing."

"Everyone loved Andrew," Helen proclaimed.

"I don't think that is true," Evelyn said. "He was rather rude to Beatrice yesterday before dinner. The poor girl looked devastated."

"Andrew finds it tiresome that Beatrice is such a frump and doesn't take care of herself." Helen gave a self-satisfied smile. "He's so proud of the way I look. I promised him I would help and give advice to Beatrice when we were married."

Helen's voice wobbled, and her eyes filled with tears once more. "Can I get you a handkerchief?"

Helen pointed at the bureau. "Top drawer, on the left-hand side."

Evelyn walked over and pulled open the drawer. She picked up a crisp white handkerchief and turned it over. In the corner, sewn in violet thread, were Helen's initials. "How beautiful. Did someone make these for you?"

"They were a gift from Andrew. I know he was sometimes a little overbearing, but he did really love me."

"I'm sure that's true," Evelyn said soothingly.

She thought of the handkerchief she found next to the Marquess's body. It was identical to the one she had just passed Helen except the one she'd hidden under a loose brick in the wall in front of the chapel was covered in blood.

26

# CHAPTER 3

ommy felt terrible leaving his mother with Evelyn, but she hadn't looked very comfortable that he was in her bedroom. Though, of course, he had sat on her bed and given her devastating news. That probably hadn't helped the situation.

The truth of the matter was that he had never once in his life been in his mother's bedroom before that day. Not even as a very young child. It simply wasn't what their family did. Rightly or wrongly, emotional situations were generally dealt with by the females in the family. He recalled an elderly aunt on his mother's side was sent for when his father died.

The year following the war had been a difficult one for Tommy. He had to come to terms with the death of his cousin, Billy, who had died a year before the war ended. Then his cousin Alice and his father had died within weeks of each other from the terrible Spanish flu that devastated an already traumatised Europe.

Tommy spent months in a military hospital after being injured in action, before he could finally come home. For a long time afterward, it was as though he and Evelyn were strangers living in the same house. She had grown accustomed to him not being about and, of course, because of the war, they had spent little of their married life together. Fortunately, their marriage had survived and got stronger. Many others when faced with the same situation had not.

As he descended the stairs, Malton opened the main door to the village vicar, John Capes. "Northmoor, how is the bride-to-be this morning?"

Tommy grimaced. "I'm afraid there will be no wedding today, John."

"No wedding?" He repeated quizzically.

"Let us talk in my office." Tommy swept his arm wide, indicating a small room on the opposite side of the entrance hall from the morning room. "Can I ask Malton to bring refreshments?"

"You know I would never say no to a good cup of coffee." John smiled, his eyes crinkling until they almost looked closed.

Tommy turned to Malton, who hovered in the doorway. "Coffee for two, My Lord?"

"Perfect, thank you."

Malton left, closing the door quietly behind him. "What has happened, Tommy?"

In public, the vicar kept up the expected terms of address between himself and Tommy, but in private Tommy had insisted they speak less formally. Over the last year, they had become extremely good friends. He felt comfortable talking to the elderly clergyman about anything, even those things that, following his service in the war, he didn't feel able to discuss with Evelyn. John listened to every horror Tommy shared, then dispensed comfort in his usual calm way.

"I'm afraid the Marquess of York has been murdered."

"Another murder in our quiet little part of the English countryside?"

"I'm afraid so." Tommy moved over to the window and opened it wide. "We do seem to attract them, don't we?"

"There is evil in everyone," John said, shaking his head sadly. "The difference is some of us choose to act on it, and some do not."

"He was rather obnoxious both before and after dinner," Tommy explained. "But should one really expect to be killed because they are not a very kind person?"

"Imagine what the man is capable of in private if he is rude in public."

Tommy nodded. "Yes, I see what you mean. If he saw no wrong in haranguing his family last night, in front of everyone, I would think he spoke to them in a far more unpleasant way when alone."

"If he's been like that for years, the list of people who disliked him could be extremely lengthy."

"The police will be thrilled," Tommy said with a wry grimace. "We have a houseful of guests, so there's plenty of people for them to interview as it is. If it turns out most of them had a reason to be happy the Marquess was dead, they will really have their work cut out for them."

"Are they on their way?"

"Yes, I called them immediately after Evelyn told me she had discovered the body. Teddy came over to confirm death, even though Evelyn said it was very clear he was deceased."

"Evelyn saw the body?" John clicked his tongue. "Sometimes I'm sure the two of you forget she is a lady. It can't do her any good to be mixed up in this type of foul mess."

Tommy laughed. "I shall let you tell my wife she should not be involved because she is female."

John flushed. "That's not exactly what I meant, Tommy, and you know it. Evelyn is a very fine young woman."

"As I said." Tommy waved a hand in the air. "I shall let her know it is your belief she should perfect her needlework, or some other genteel pastime instead of investigating murders."

"You know I worry about both of you," John said eventually.

Malton knocked on the door before entering with a tray of coffee. The cook, Mrs O'Connell, had placed several biscuits and small pastries on a plate. "Cook said she wasn't sure what we would do about lunch, so thought you would appreciate a little something to keep you going."

John patted his stomach. "Please pass on my thanks to your cook. The dear lady is well aware of my weakness for her sweets."

"How is Violet's cooking these days?"

The vicar picked up a shortbread biscuit as Malton unobtrusively left the room. "Her meals are much improved, but I don't think she will ever master the art of the food types I really enjoy."

"Cakes, biscuits, and puddings?"

"Precisely." John dabbed at the corner of his mouth with a napkin. "This shortbread, for instance, simply melts in the mouth."

"You don't need to convince me. It's simply delicious, isn't it?" Tommy picked up a biscuit.

"I'm shocked you are not the size of a barn living in this house."

"The amount of walking I do around the estate helps to keep me trim, I believe." Tommy looked down at his waistline. "Other than baking, Violet has worked out well for you?"

John's previous housekeeper left a lot to be desired and had left his employ at Tommy's urging. Violet Cross had lived with her brother, Alfred, in the village after her husband had been killed in action. Alfred received a prison sentence for his part in a murder committed in the village's churchyard, leaving Violet with no home or income. Tommy and Evelyn had arranged for Violet to work for John, who didn't mind that she needed to bring her young children with her to the vicarage.

"She is a very sweet young woman," John confirmed. "And her children are delightful."

Tommy breathed out a sigh of relief. "After I meddled so terribly, that is good to hear."

"It may interest you to know something." John's blue eyes twinkled and Tommy knew he was about to hear a piece of village gossip. "Your estate manager has been seen in the village paying calls on Ellen Armstrong."

"Is that right?" Tommy grinned behind his teacup. "How marvellous. Ellen is a lovely young woman."

"Giving young Partridge a chance has worked out very well for you, hasn't it?"

"He has never given me a moment's regret," Tommy agreed. "Even though it's not at all his job, he didn't even blink when I asked him to position himself at the head of our drive and let guests know the wedding was off, and they were not to come to the house."

"Police orders?" John commiserated.

"Yes, no one in, no one out they said. Obviously, I allowed you in because I thought you would be needed." Tommy glanced out of the window. "Here are the detectives now."

Moments later, the police were announced by Malton and John excused himself from the room.

"Detective Inspector Andrews." Tommy extended a hand. "It's nice to see you again, though I am sorry it has to be under such difficult circumstances."

The policeman reluctantly shook Tommy's hand and took the seat opposite Tommy. "Lord Northmoor, I thought it prudent to set some ground rules before I take a look at the body."

"Of course," Tommy said amiably. He knew what was to come: don't interfere in the police investigation, do share information, and particularly don't pretend you're still a detective and solve the murder before the real police.

"I know that you and Lady Northmoor enjoy investigating murders." The detective folded his hands in his lap, as though trying to keep them still and prevent himself from gesticulating at Tommy. "But after last time, I would implore you to stay out of it. That lunatic could have badly hurt your wife."

"I have just been discussing the same topic with the vicar." Tommy steepled his hands on his desk. "My wife is not the sort of woman who does well with someone telling her what to do."

Detective Inspector Andrews gave Tommy a long, searching look. He clearly believed a man could, and should, give his wife instructions and expect to be obeyed. Especially when that man was one of a certain power.

Tommy wished the detective would realise that he was a man just like himself—the title and the grand house were his only by a quirk of fate. They could easily belong to someone else if life had worked out differently.

"Is everyone that was here yesterday still in the house?"

"Everyone except Hugh Norton-Cavendish. I'm afraid he received news yesterday that his father had passed away. Hugh left before dinner."

"I read about it in the newspaper this morning. Terrible business."

"Yes, Hugh has become a very dear family friend. He was most distressed."

"If anything else changes, or you find anything out through the little chats you and your wife are so keen on conducting, I will expect you to keep me informed."

"You have my word." Tommy nodded. "I suppose you will want to use this room again for your investigation, and for interviewing our guests?"

"That would be very acceptable, My Lord."

Tommy stood and moved over to the door. "Of course. I shall have refreshments sent in to you. Where is your deputy?"

Detective Inspector Andrews pointed to the top of the drive. "He has taken over from your estate manager. I have stationed uniformed police at various points outside the grounds to ensure no one escapes."

Tommy did not take time to point out that if someone wanted to run away after killing the Marquess, they had plenty of time to do so since his death. No doubt he would work that out for himself when he saw the body—the doctor had said it was clear the Marquess of York had been dead for hours.

~

*A*fter Helen eventually told Evelyn she wanted to be alone 'with her thoughts of Andrew', Evelyn made her way downstairs.

"Who is Tommy with?" She whispered to Malton, who stood tall and sentry-like outside Tommy's office.

"The police detective from York," he whispered back.

"Then I shall not disturb him." Evelyn walked away from Malton before turning back to him. "Have you seen Harry at all this morning?"

"I'm afraid not, My Lady."

Evelyn grimaced. It was the answer she was expecting, but not the one she wanted. "If Tommy is looking for me, I shall be in the kitchen. If anyone else wants me, please take as long as you can to find me."

Malton inclined his head. "As you wish, My Lady."

Evelyn hurried toward the back stairs that led down to the kitchen. Turning up in the manor's kitchen was not unusual for Evelyn. When she had first done it the previous year, before she was Lady Northmoor, the cook, Mrs O'Connell, was outraged. The staff were all now well accustomed to her popping down for a chat.

"Ooh, Lady Northmoor!" Nora, the kitchen maid, exclaimed as she entered the busy room.

One of the parlour maids jumped to her feet, her quick action sloshing tea from her cup into the saucer underneath. Evelyn raised her hand level to her body and then lowered it. "Sit down and finish your tea before it gets cold. Please don't feel that you need to leave the kitchen on my account."

"You always seem to know when I've got something to tell you," Nora said. The young girl was so exuberant she was practically hopping from foot to foot as though the stone floor was burning her feet.

Mrs O'Connell placed two cups of tea at the end of the huge wooden table that dominated the busy room. I'll join you in a cup of tea if I may, My Lady? My poor old feet are killing me after all the extra work of the last few days."

"Oh yes, that would be wonderful. A pleasant chat with friends is exactly what I need." Evelyn took a seat and glanced over at the cook. "You do look rather tired, Mrs O'Connell."

"I don't mind telling you, My Lady, I'm absolutely jiggered." Nora looked hopefully at the cook, her eyes bright with excitement. "Yes, Nora, you can join us."

Nora grinned and poured herself a cup of tea. "Thank you, Cook, I'm very grateful."

"Well, it's not as though you'd be getting any work done, is it? You've been like a child at Christmas all morning."

Evelyn hid a smile. Although the cook pretended that Nora's endless stream of chattering got on her nerves, she was very fond of her young kitchen maid. "What do you have to tell me, Nora?"

"Well, My Lady, it's like this." Nora began. "Albert has only gone and popped the question!"

"Oh my goodness, Nora, I'm so thrilled for you!" Evelyn leaned closer to Nora. "Has he given you a ring?"

Nora lifted her left hand to display a simple gold band. "It's nothing fancy, but Albert saved for months to afford a ring. I think it's the most beautiful thing I've ever seen."

"I agree," Evelyn said. "It's perfect. I do hope Albert knows how lucky he is?"

Nora blushed. "He says it might be awhile before we can marry, as he has to save for somewhere to live. He doesn't want us starting our married life living with his parents."

"I will have a word with Lord Northmoor," Evelyn said decisively. "There are several cottages on the estate that are empty. I'm certain he would rent one to you and Albert for a very reasonable price."

"Oh Lady Northmoor, do you think he would, really?" Nora's hand rose to cover her mouth, and her eyes filled with tears. "I'd be ever so grateful, and so would Albert."

"Hard work should be rewarded, and I know Lord Northmoor believes that too. I shall speak to him as soon as I can and see what we can arrange."

"I'm so happy I could kiss you!"

"Nora!" Mrs O'Connell said sharply. "Get a hold of yourself and dry those tears, you daft ha'p'orth."

Nora produced a handkerchief from her apron pocket and wiped her eyes. "Did you want to ask us something, Lady Northmoor? We heard you found the Marquess over in the chapel dead as a doornail."

"I'm afraid that's right, Nora." Evelyn leaned closer to the two women and lowered her voice. "Unfortunately, it seems that no one has seen Master Harry since last night. Might he have popped down here this morning to satisfy his sweet tooth?"

"I haven't seen him," Mrs O'Connell confirmed. "What about you, Nora? Polly?"

The young parlour maid looked up at the sound of her

name. An expression of fear crossed her face before she spoke. "I ain't seen a thing."

"It's quite alright," Evelyn said gently. "No one is in any trouble, nor shall they be, but I simply must find Harry before the police realise he is missing."

"Master Harry is a nice young fella," Mrs O'Connell said. "You surely can't be thinking he has anything to do with the Marquess's death?"

"Of course not," Evelyn replied quickly. "I don't think so, but the police might not see it that way."

"Yes, I see that." The cook nodded. "Girls, please ask around the staff, discreetly like, to see if anyone has seen Master Harry. I'm sure Lord Northmoor would be very grateful to know where his brother is."

Nora and Polly nodded, the latter immediately jumping to her feet. "I'd better get back to work before Mrs Chapman comes looking for me."

"Discreetly, remember, Polly!" Mrs O'Connell called as the young girl left the kitchen as though she herself were being chased by the police.

"She's a good girl," Nora said. "I think she's just very nervous around you, My Lady. She's not used to your visits to the kitchen like I am."

"Just you remember your place, my girl." The cook admonished.

"You'll let me know as soon as Harry is located?"

Mrs O'Connell nodded. "We'll get word to you as soon as he's found. I'm sure he's sleeping off the skinful he had last night. Nothing to worry about."

Evelyn bit her lip. "I hope you're right, Mrs O'Connell, I really do."

"*L*ord Northmoor, might I have a word?" David Ryder approached Tommy, looking very apologetic.

"Of course, David. Let's go into the billiard room. There shouldn't be anyone else around at this time of day." Tommy waited until David closed the door behind him before speaking again. "Is there something wrong?"

"Not wrong, exactly, but this is a very sensitive issue." David looked away, clearly ill at ease.

David's demeanour confused Tommy. For the last few months, they had worked together closely on business matters. Until recently, David had worked as a solicitor in London. Partly because of his new relationship with Tommy's cousin, Madeleine, but mostly because of personal reasons he had left London and set up practice in York.

"Does this have something to do with the death of the Marquess?"

"Not directly." David glanced at Tommy before looking at the closed door of the billiard room. "That is...what I am about to ask may appear in jolly poor taste."

"Best to simply say what it is, man."

"It seems rather a shame for all the food and preparations to go to waste," David said earnestly. "I wondered if...I know it's horribly presumptuous of me...but would there be a possibility of you allowing Madeleine and me to marry at the chapel? Obviously not today...we would have to get a Special Licence, of course...but perhaps tomorrow or Monday?"

"What does Madeleine think of this idea?" Tommy peered at his friend's face closely. David had yet to meet his eyes. "You have spoken to her about this, I hope?"

David cleared his throat. "It was actually her idea."

Tommy chuckled. "Was it really? Perhaps I was wrong thinking she was the more timid of the two sisters."

"Oh, she is," David said sincerely. "It's just that we've fallen hopelessly in love. I never dared hope she would come to love me as much as I knew I loved her when we were in

London, but she assures me she has. After Georges, I was prepared to wait for as long as she needed, just so long as she gave me some hope."

Madeleine's sweetheart, Georges, had been killed earlier that year at Tommy's London home in Belgrave Square He and Evelyn had solved the murder, as they had several others previously. "It seems rather quick, but if you're both sure, I certainly have no objections. I wouldn't have the first idea what is to be done about a Special Licence though."

"My brother knows someone who has the Archbishop of Canterbury's ear," David said, his cheeks flushing. "I know this seems like I have come to you with a fait accompli, but I wanted to be certain it was possible before I asked."

"Is that all that is required? The Archbishop's ear?"

"One has to pay a sum of money."

"Go ahead with your plans," Tommy said decisively. "I shall speak to the vicar on your behalf. It may be best if you plan to marry in the village church rather than here at the chapel. My agreement to your suggestion is on the basis that neither my mother nor the police have any objections."

"I have every faith in you to solve the murder before the day is out."

"Steady on, old chap."

"I've seen you and Lady Northmoor at work, remember?" David grinned, all awkwardness now gone. "Where is your wife, by the way?"

"I left her with my mother." Tommy raised an eyebrow. "But you're right, the chances of Evelyn being upstairs comforting Mother and not looking for clues or interrogating people are incredibly slim."

"She is a very admirable woman. It seems to be a trait common to Christie women."

Tommy could not disagree. Although he had met his cousins for the first time when they returned from France some months earlier, he liked both Madeleine and Elise very much.

"I should probably excuse myself and find out what my wife is up to," Tommy said with a wry smile. "If only to remind her we are a team, and she shouldn't be wandering off by herself with a murderer on the loose."

"It is rather alarming, isn't it?" David leaned forward in his chair. "Do you have any early suspects?"

"I don't know the Marquess's family at all. I met them for the first time yesterday, the same with Frank and Jane Simmons. Obviously I've known Sir Richard for years."

"He is your mother's godfather?" David's brow furrowed in concentration. "I'm certain I've seen him before."

Tommy grinned. "I'm sure you will have come across him in London. He rarely comes to the country. He much prefers the gentleman's clubs in the city."

"Yes, I'm sure that must be it." David looked doubtful.

"He was highly decorated in the Boer War. Perhaps you've seen his picture in the newspapers, he's given lots of interviews over the years." Tommy shrugged. "In any case, I'm sure it'll come back to you."

David got to his feet. "I'll let Madeleine know what we've discussed. Thank you, I appreciate your consideration."

Tommy accepted David's outstretched hand and shook it. He would be a welcome addition to the family. But before they could enjoy the happy occasion, he needed to solve the murder currently hanging over the house like a cloud of doom.

# CHAPTER 4

*E*velyn marched over to her bedroom door as soon as Tommy opened it. "Hurry!"

Tommy looked around, his expression bewildered, as Evelyn pulled him inside. "Why are you in such a rush?"

"I don't want Detective Inspector Andrews to catch us."

"In our own bedroom?" Tommy's face immediately showed his amusement. "Heavens, we will be arrested on the spot."

"This is serious, Tommy!" Evelyn said sternly. "Your brother is missing."

"What exactly do you mean by missing?" Tommy sat on the edge of their bed.

"Missing." Evelyn threw her hands in the air. "No one has seen him since after dinner last night."

"You don't think?" Tommy frowned at her. "You can't think he had something to do with the Marquess's death?"

"I certainly don't think so." Evelyn stopped pacing and stood opposite Tommy. "But you do remember what happened when your Uncle Charles was poisoned? You were the primary suspect."

"But Harry…"

"Adored his father and most likely was as keen on your mother marrying Andrew as you were."

Tommy rested his elbow on his knee and let his head fall into his upturned palm. "Yes, I see what you mean."

"Mrs Chapman has instructed the maids to check any empty rooms. Partridge is outside checking the grounds as unobtrusively as he can."

Tommy raised his head. "You've been rather busy organising things."

"Of course. The question is, what are we to do now?"

"Does Mother know?"

"Constance checked with her. Neither she, nor your mother, nor Grace have seen him since dinner."

"The little fool." Tommy shook his head. "He had a lot to drink. Likely he'll be sleeping it off somewhere."

"Everyone has arrived at the same conclusion." Evelyn rested a hand on Tommy's shoulder. "But where?"

"Has anyone checked the stables?"

"First place Partridge checked. Doris has even given the dogs one of Harry's pullovers and taken them outside to see if they could track him."

Tommy smiled despite his obvious worry. "Your dogs are not bloodhounds."

"They are not," Evelyn agreed. "But they are very sensitive and intelligent animals. That awful noise Nancy made before I found the Marquess is still ringing in my ears."

"You poor darling." Tommy caught hold of Evelyn's hand and pulled her onto his knee. "We haven't really had much opportunity to talk about the murder scene until now. Do you feel able to discuss it now?"

Evelyn pulled back slightly so she could look directly into Tommy's face. "You are talking to me, your wife, not some silly little ninny who faints at the sight of a drop of blood."

"He was on the floor, near the altar, on his back?"

She closed her eyes so she could picture things exactly as

she had seen them and report back accurately to Tommy. "That's correct. The knife appeared to be sticking in his stomach above where I imagine his umbilicus was. Of course, I did not adjust his clothing to check, so that is a guess. The knife looked old."

"Why do you say old?"

Evelyn thought for a moment. "Perhaps not old, but not cared for. Tarnished, like it had been kept in an outbuilding where it was dusty and forgotten."

"That suggests the murder was a spur-of-the-moment act. There was a meeting arranged, and the murderer grabbed a weapon in case it was needed."

"Can we say it's a spur of the moment deed if the villain took a weapon with him to a purported meeting?" Evelyn didn't necessarily disagree with Tommy, but it was important they explore all aspects of the crime rather than make erroneous assumptions.

"I suppose it's not a sudden loss of control, otherwise he would've seized something nearby. Like one of those loose bricks on the wall around the chapel."

"I wondered if you'd remember those." Evelyn put up her left hand and waggled her thumb. "Harry is missing. The murderer took a weapon to the chapel."

"What is point three? Why have you stopped talking?"

"This is a little awkward, but what is done is done."

"Evelyn? What is done?"

"Next to Andrew's body there was a rather pretty handkerchief. I picked it up without thinking."

"But you put it right back down where you found it?"

"I'm afraid I did not. The hankie was embroidered in one corner with someone's initials."

"Evelyn, don't keep me in suspense. Whose initials?"

"The initials were H.C."

"Helen Christie."

"When I was in your mother's bedroom earlier, I had an

opportunity to get a fresh handkerchief out of her drawer. It was the same as the one I found. She said they were a gift from Andrew."

"Well, that explains it then." Tommy exhaled loudly. "Maybe he kept hold of one for himself, to remind him of Mother."

"Good golly, Tommy, you don't really believe that, do you?"

He grinned wryly. "No, not really. Where is the hankie now?"

"Those loose bricks you were talking about? I stuffed it in underneath one."

"Why did you do that?"

"I panicked," Evelyn said honestly. "Nancy was howling, Andrew was dead, and there was your mother's hankie covered in blood."

"You didn't say it was bloody." Tommy shook his head. "Whose blood do you think it is?"

"I expect it is Andrew's, and the killer used the hankie to wipe his hands clean. The knife was pushed up to the hilt, so it's likely the murderer had blood on his hands."

Tommy shuddered. "It must be very sharp."

"Or the murderer extremely powerful."

"What is point four?"

"I suppose, as it always is, the unknown. At the start of our investigations there are things we know, then there is information we discover, but there's also the unknown and we must discover that to unravel the mystery and unmask the killer."

"Do you think anyone will be sad the Marquess is dead?"

"I shouldn't think so," Evelyn said matter-of-factly. "But that doesn't mean he deserved to die."

"Perhaps the unknown in this case is the heir," Tommy suggested.

"Who is the heir to the Marquess of York?"

"I spoke to Sir Richard about it. He spends so much time in his clubs in London, he knows everyone and everything. Sir Richard suggested there is a cousin in India, but he wasn't certain."

It made perfect sense. "So point four is the unknown heir. It could be anyone. For all we know, the heir could be present in the house now."

"I shall speak to Frank Simmons. He was to be the Marquess's best man. Surely, he should know the identity of the heir? Perhaps he can tell me a little more about Andrew, too. All we know is what we saw yesterday evening, and it wasn't very flattering."

"Perhaps there's nothing good to know about him." Evelyn rested her head against Tommy's shoulder. "Some people are simply not very nice."

"Sir Richard also said something very interesting. He wondered why the Marquess was marrying my mother and not a younger woman who could provide him with his own successor instead of the estate going to distant relatives."

"I would say that's obvious."

"Is it?" Tommy lifted one knee and Evelyn raised her head in response. "Why?"

"Quite clearly, he was marrying your mother to try and get his hands on as much of your fortune as possible. Really, Tommy, sometimes you are incredibly naïve."

"When did you become so very wise, my darling?"

Evelyn leaned forward and pressed her lips to Tommy's. "The moment I married you."

"I could stay here like this with you all day," Tommy murmured against her hair.

"But we can't because there's yet another murderer on the loose, your mother is distraught, and your brother is missing."

"That about sums it up. I'll seek Frank Simmons, and

perhaps you could talk to his wife? If he doesn't want to speak ill about his dead chum, perhaps his wife might?"

She wrapped her arms around her husband's neck and drew him close. "One more kiss for luck. Then we shall get to work."

"A good husband should never disagree with his wife." Tommy grinned at her. "Especially when he has a wife that is so very wonderful."

~

Tommy left their bedroom after Evelyn. A twinge of conscience told him he should head straight for Detective Inspector Andrews and let him know Harry hadn't been seen for over twelve hours. His loyalty toward his brother was the more powerful emotion, and he determined to speak with Frank Simmons first. If Harry hadn't been found by lunchtime, he would let the detective know.

After a quick consultation with Malton, who knew everything there was to know, he headed to the billiard room. The doors to the room that had always struck Tommy as being old fashioned and rather stuffy were open to the garden. The Marquess's best man had carried a chair outside and placed it on the small paved patio.

Tommy followed the other man's lead and placed his chair opposite Frank. "Morning."

"Northmoor." Frank removed the pipe from his mouth and tapped the bowl on the ashtray next to him. "Absolutely dreadful news. Can it really be murder?"

"I'm afraid it looks like it." Tommy confirmed. "The police have arrived from York. The fellow in charge, Detective Inspector Andrews, will want to speak to everyone."

"He can't possibly suspect one of us?" Frank jabbed a thumb toward his chest, as though the thought that the killer was one of the guests had only just occurred to him.

"I suppose it's possible someone came onto the estate last night, killed the Marquess, then made off. But it's not very likely."

"It seems the most obvious answer to me," Frank argued stubbornly.

"A stranger lacks the requisite motive."

"Ah." Frank waved his pipe in the air. "But that's not necessarily true, is it? What if Andrew came upon some sort of illicit activity and they killed him to keep the enterprise secret?"

Tommy mused over the possibility, thinking about the previous year when he had discovered his estate manager and a villager had run a poaching scheme on the estate. Now that villager, Geoffrey Beckett, worked for Tommy to keep poachers off his land. "You're right. That is a possibility."

"You don't sound very convinced."

"Was the Marquess the type of man to have enemies?"

Frank shook his head and looked morosely at Tommy. "Now that's a question."

"Will you answer it for me?"

"We were friends, of a sort." Frank looked off across the lawn. "He wasn't the easiest of men. Most people put up with him because of who he was."

"Including you?"

"The hunting on his estate was always top notch, and when he wasn't being boorish, he could be a fairly decent chap." Frank replied defensively.

That wasn't the most favourable character reference Tommy had ever heard. "And when he was being impolite?"

Frank turned back to Tommy. "Then he was a thoroughly nasty fellow."

"Horrid enough that someone may want to kill him?"

"I say," Frank said. "Aren't you rather doing the police's job for them?"

Tommy glanced back at the house. "This is my home. I

cannot help but feel a little responsible for what happens in it. My mother asked me and Lady Northmoor to host her wedding here. Now her fiancé is dead. You can understand why I have taken this dastardly crime personally, I hope?"

"Of course, yes." Frank stuffed the bowl of his pipe with tobacco from the pouch resting on his lap. He then tamped it down and struck a match. "That makes sense."

"Do excuse me for a moment." Tommy went back into the billiard room and returned momentarily with a cigar. "I rarely smoke. But I find it helps me to think."

"Helps me relax," Frank said.

Tommy lit his cigar and exhaled a satisfying plume of smoke into the summer air. "You suggested Andrew could have come across some sort of shady deal last night. What do you think he was doing wandering about late at night?"

Frank shrugged. "It was a warm night. Perhaps he was just taking a stroll. Maybe he was nervous about the wedding and couldn't sleep."

"Could he have met someone?"

"I dare say anything is possible. I was to be the fellow's best man, but as I've already told you, we were not friends. At least, not in the conventional sense."

Tommy tested out another theory. "Might he have been so rude to someone they were driven to kill him?"

"It would seem jolly ridiculous to meet someone you had insulted that badly out in the dark all alone," Frank said reasonably. "I don't think Andrew was a foolhardy man."

"Who is his heir?" Tommy changed the direction of his questions.

"Goodness." Frank sucked on the stem of his pipe. "I'm afraid I don't know. That would certainly be a powerful motive wouldn't it?"

"I've heard it suggested there might be a cousin in India who would inherit?"

"It's not the sort of thing Andrew would ever discuss with me."

Tommy nodded in understanding. "Not that type of friend."

"Indeed." Frank frowned. "I'm not actually sure the estate would be worth killing for."

"The Marquess had financial problems?"

"Again, I do not know this because I was in Andrew's confidence." Frank leaned forward as though he was about to impart crucial information. "It's more a feeling I have, now I think about it. Before you asked the question, I hadn't given the matter any considerable thought. When you suggested Andrew may have been killed for his estate, and I considered that suggestion, it just seems wrong to me."

"Do you have reasons you can share about your feelings?"

"The obvious one is that the house is very much as it has been for decades." Frank leaned back and crossed one leg over the other. Tommy thought about the main rooms in Hessleham Hall—they were just as they had been since he was a young boy. "Some rooms are closed up, and the staff seems a little skeletal for such a large house. One always sees the same faces carrying out a range of duties. We have more at my own modest estate."

It was interesting information, but not proof of the Marquess's financial position. Perhaps the man had simply been miserly? Though it could explain why he was happy having his wedding hosted by his fiancée's dead husband's family. That had always seemed rather peculiar to Tommy. He would have to ask his mother whose idea that was.

"My own home has been unchanged for years."

"Hessleham Hall does not look unkempt in any way, Lord Northmoor. It's a beautiful, well-maintained house." Frank re-lit his pipe. "As I've said, it's very difficult to explain exactly what I mean. It's simply a feeling I got about the Marquess's home."

"Perhaps his daughters would have a better idea of their father's situation."

Frank almost choked as he simultaneously drew on his pipe and laughed. "Goodness gracious, no, Lord Northmoor. The girls will not have any idea of their father's financial position. They are as scared of him as their poor dead mother was."

"What happened to the Marchioness?"

"Took to her bed when Frances was around four years old. She would occasionally attend a dinner if Andrew was entertaining, but she rarely accompanied him to any events outside the house. For instance, she never travelled with him to London. She stayed in the country with the girls. My understanding is she had some sort of heart issue. Died a year or so ago."

"How tragic," Tommy murmured, feeling desperately sorry for a woman he hadn't even met, and sorrier still for Beatrice and Frances, who had been left with a cold and unfeeling father.

They were distracted from their conversation by a dog who streaked across the lawn and came to a stop near Tommy, his tongue lolling out of his mouth and onto Tommy's shoes. He leaned forward and stroked the dog's majestic head. "Now, Davey, it's always lovely to see you, but I'm certain you shouldn't be out here alone."

"You're talking to that animal as though he is human."

"My wife prizes her dogs as much as any human." Tommy grinned. "I rather think her treatment of her dogs has rubbed off on me. I must admit they have become a part of my family."

"Lady Northmoor is a very modern young woman."

"She is," Tommy agreed. "And I am inordinately proud of her and the way she has taken to her new and unexpected role."

"If you don't mind my saying, it is clear yours is very much a love match."

Tommy did not put propriety before praise of his wife. "Yes, we are very lucky to have found each other."

"You should bear in mind that not everyone is so fortunate." Frank tapped his pipe into the ashtray. "I don't believe your mother and Andrew would have had a happy marriage."

"Lady Northmoor believes the Marquess was marrying my mother because he believed that would give him access to some of my money."

Frank looked away. "I wouldn't have presumed to have spoken as plainly as that. But I believe Lady Northmoor is very close to the mark with her understanding of the situation."

Doris, Evelyn's maid, rounded the corner of the house and hurried over to them. Her face was flushed from the sun, which shone proudly in a cloudless sky. "Lord Northmoor, I'm terribly sorry."

"I see he's slipped his lead again."

"He has a talent for it, My Lord." Doris fastened the lead around the dog's neck. "The silly animal seems happy to lie directly in the sun even though he must be boiling."

Tommy held out his hand. "I shall take him back inside when I've finished out here."

Doris bobbed her knee. "As you wish, My Lord."

He would take Davey for an extended walk around the estate. Not even Detective Inspector Andrews could criticise him for exercising his dog.

Frank Simmons seemed an honest sort of fellow, but Tommy considered he hadn't really learned anything new from the man. Finding his brother must take priority—if no one else had found him, he must try himself.

*J*ane Simmons was seated in one of the comfortable chairs in the library. Although she had a book resting on her lap, she looked out wistfully across the lawn.

"Mrs Simmons?" Evelyn walked into the room. "May I join you?"

"Oh, Lady Northmoor, you startled me!" Jane blushed. "Of course you may join me. It's your house. Do come in and sit down."

The older woman was what Aunt Em would call a 'twitterer'—the kind of woman who said entirely too many words when one or two would suffice. She even looked a little like a bird with her sharp, angular body and beak-shaped nose.

Evelyn pulled one of the heavy leather chairs closer to Jane and sat down. "Shall I ring for tea?"

"Oh!" Jane peered toward the clock on the mantle. "It isn't tea time, is it? We haven't had lunch."

"I don't always follow conventions," Evelyn said. "If I want tea, or my guests do, we have tea."

"Goodness!" One of Jane's hands flew to her chest as though having tea at any time of day was one of the most shocking things she had ever heard. "How very odd. But simply lovely, of course, if you like tea. Which I do."

Evelyn despaired of finding out anything useful from the woman. She started every sentence she spoke with a wide-eyed stare and looked completely stupefied. "Then I shall ring for a tray."

She walked over to the fireplace and pulled the bell cord to the side, then returned to her seat. Evelyn could feel Jane's eyes on her every step of the way. She smiled reassuringly at the other woman as she sat back down.

Jane blinked rapidly, her hands fluttering in her lap as though she wasn't at all sure what to do with them. The book

51

she hadn't been reading fell to the floor, and Jane's face flushed beet red. "Oh! How clumsy of me."

Evelyn leaned forward at the same time as Jane, and their foreheads bumped together. "Oops a daisy. I beg your pardon."

"Lady Northmoor! I'm mortified! I am such a bumbling fool. Can you ever forgive me?"

To Evelyn's astonishment, tears balanced precariously on the other woman's eyelashes, and she bit her lip as though attempting to hold back her distress. "There's nothing to forgive. Mrs Simmons, I am every bit as much to blame for that little accident as you. There's no harm done." Evelyn retrieved the book and looked at the cover. "I adore The Secret Garden. Have you read it before?"

"Many times," Jane answered quietly.

"Please," Evelyn said gently. "You must try to relax. If I didn't know better, I'd think you were dreadfully afraid of me."

"I am rather," Jane replied, then slapped a hand over her mouth. "Goodness! I don't know why I said that."

"Perhaps it's true?" Evelyn tried to read Jane's expression, then came to a stunning realisation. "You are afraid of me."

"Not afraid as such." Jane anxiously twisted her hands in her lap. "Perhaps just a little awed."

Evelyn could barely believe her ears. "Of me?"

"You're very beautiful."

"Thank you, that's very kind." Evelyn passed the book back over to Jane. "But I refuse to allow you to be afraid of me based on how I look. I promise I'm a jolly pleasant person when you get to know me."

"Oh no!" Jane shook her head vehemently. "I couldn't possibly imagine getting to know someone like you."

The maid Evelyn remembered as Polly arrived at the door to the library, looking every bit as nervous as Mrs Simmons. When had people started being scared to talk to her? In her mind, she was still the same person she had always been—plain old Evelyn Hamilton, as was, who lived in the village with her parents. Her father was a member of parliament and her eccentric mother thought much more of her dogs than her own children.

She had tried hard to throw herself into doing things that were befitting to a 'lady of the manor,' but perhaps she had forgotten that she needed to show people more of herself, so they felt more comfortable around her.

"Ah, Polly, isn't it?" Evelyn smiled warmly at the young girl.

"Yes, My Lady." The girl bobbed her knee, her face red, and legs visibly shaking.

"Will you ask Cook if she would prepare a tea tray for Mrs Simmons and me? And maybe some of her delightful short-bread, if the vicar hasn't eaten it all?"

"Of course, My Lady. Right away."

Polly fled from the room and Evelyn sighed. "Am I really so terrifying?"

"You're Lady Northmoor," Jane Simmons said as though that was enough.

"I'm still a young woman who likes to have friends she can talk to."

"Oh! I couldn't…"

Evelyn held up a hand. "I refuse to listen to you telling me you cannot be my friend. We most certainly can."

"The Marquess…" Jane cleared her throat. "The Marquess was very clear about his place in society and ours."

"But your husband was to be his best man." Evelyn frowned. "I don't understand."

"It's like this." Jane leaned forward, suddenly looking more excited than frightened. "He was a frightful bully."

"The Marquess was very unkind to his daughters last night," Evelyn said carefully.

"He was unpleasant to everyone!" Jane's hands spread

wide as though the room were full of people. "I know it's very poor form to speak ill of the dead, but Lady Northmoor, no one deserved to be killed more than that man."

Evelyn's lips parted in surprise that the meek Jane would say such a thing. She struggled to find an answer that wouldn't agree with Jane's remark but would encourage her to say more. "Really?"

"He was positively vile to poor Frank."

"Was he?" Evelyn shook her head, trying to clear her thoughts. "I assumed they were great chums."

"Frank enjoyed being included in the Marquess's inner circle." Jane put a hand over her mouth again, but this time to stifle a girlish giggle. "I say circle...but really they were hangers on. Snobs that accepted an invitation from him only because he was a Marquess."

"He didn't have any real friends?"

"Absolutely not. Enemies, I should say. And lots of them."

"I don't suppose you have any idea who could have killed him then?"

Jane laughed gaily. "Oh, Lady Northmoor, I should think it could be almost anyone who ever met the man."

Polly returned with the tea tray and Evelyn decided she would ask Jane to help her with one of her many charities. The last thing she wanted was for the women of the county to think she was such a grand lady that she was unapproachable. She hoped it was only the Marquess's influence on Jane that gave her such an impression, and it wasn't what others thought of her.

Evelyn considered that if she had one fault it was caring too much about others' opinions of her. She shouldn't care whether or not people liked her, but she couldn't help it.

# CHAPTER 5

"*L*ady Beatrice, may I say how desperately sorry I am about your father." Tommy approached the Marquess's eldest daughter, Lady Beatrice Dawson.

Beatrice looked up from her seat on a wooden bench at the far end of the manor house's lawn. She had chosen a shady spot that wasn't visible from the house. "I shouldn't think anyone is really sorry."

"My mother…"

Beatrice's dark eyes fastened onto Tommy's with sudden fervour. "Your mother wanted to be a Marchioness. I don't believe she had any affection for my father."

"I'm sure that's not true." Tommy felt honour bound to defend his mother.

"Ask your sister," Beatrice said in a bored voice.

"Constance?"

"Rather unfortunate, but I overheard her talking to Lord Chesden about your mother's desire to be a higher rank than your wife."

Tommy wondered how the conversation he had hoped to start about the Marquess of York, and who could have killed

55

him, had got out of hand so very quickly. "My wife isn't the least bit interested in titles."

"I'm sure that's true." Beatrice looked away from Tommy, and toward the river that shimmered in the summer sunlight. "But your sister was very convincing in her discussion with Lord Chesden regarding your mother's intentions."

"Where did this conversation take place?" Tommy resisted the urge to race back to the house and ask Constance herself why she was giving such a fellow as shallow as Alexander Ryder any attention at all. Only months earlier, he'd fancied himself in love with Tommy's cousin Elise.

"That's the unfortunate part." Beatrice sounded embarrassed and her hands twisted together in her lap. "I was sitting in one of the high-backed chairs in the billiard room when your sister and Lord Chesden entered the room. I didn't alert them to my presence, so I overheard every word."

"Please accept my sincere apologies on behalf of my sister if her indiscreet comments upset you."

Beatrice laughed, a harsh sound devoid of any humour. "I couldn't care less if your mother was marrying my father only to become a Marchioness. It makes no difference to me or my sister. Frances and I are adults. It's not as though your mother would be our stepmother in anything other than name."

"There is something I am confused about," Tommy said, hoping his impertinent question would catch Beatrice off guard and she would answer it honestly. "My mother suggested that you and Lady Frances lived independently of your father, but I understand you all live in the Manor House on the Marquess's estate. How can those two facts be reconciled?"

"Oh, that's very simple." Beatrice's mouth twisted into a self-deprecating smile. "My husband has independent means. His family own several coal mines. Leslie's father gave each of his sons a coal mine to run when they married. Les's has been extremely profitable. He pays a rather decent salary to Frances's husband to manage the place for him."

"Your father was very nasty to you last night," Tommy said softly. "Didn't you ever want to leave your father's house and live somewhere else with your husband, given he had the finances to make it possible?"

"We stayed, Frances and I, because of our mother. We would never have left her in the house with our father."

"She died last year?"

"Mother had been unwell for years." Beatrice gazed at Tommy, then looked away again, but not before he had seen the sheen of tears in her eyes. "I think Father's cruelty eventually wore her down, and she didn't want to live, even for Frances and me, and her grandchildren."

"I don't think I realised your father was a grandfather." Tommy pursed his lips together. How had it come to the day his mother was supposed to marry, and he knew so little about her fiancé? Had he become so busy in his own life he had neglected his mother and siblings that badly?

"I have two children, George and Margaret. Frances has a little girl named Dorothy. We left them at home with their nanny."

Could it be possible that George was the heir to the Marquess of York through his father? Tommy debated phrasing the question carefully, but Beatrice had seemed very open in their conversation so he decided to just ask her outright what he wanted to know.

"Do you know who the heir to your father's estate is?"

"I'm afraid I do not know."

"Your father wasn't keen to establish an heir presumptive?"

"I suppose he thought he was young enough that he had years before that became an issue."

Tommy assumed the Marquess of York to be a little older

than his mother, in his early sixties. "He would not secure an heir by marrying my mother."

"No." Beatrice turned to Tommy, her face sad. "But he would see that marriage as securing his family finances."

Had Evelyn been right, and the Marquess was only marrying his mother for money? It seemed Beatrice was of the same opinion. "I still don't fully understand. Please forgive me, but you've just told me your husband has independent means."

"He owns a coal mine outright, in his own name," Beatrice explained. "The rest of his family fortune is held in a trust by his father, who is as healthy as you and I. Father couldn't get his hands on any of Les's family money, no matter how hard he tried."

Tommy was appalled. "He tried?"

"Oh, certainly he did. He was forever inviting Les's father to Yorkville Manor and making both veiled and completely overt suggestions that he increase Les's allowance." Beatrice smiled. "I think the old man deliberately gave his sons property so my father couldn't get money out of Les."

Beatrice's words whirled around Tommy's head. "What about your sister's husband?"

"It's not really the done thing to talk about the finances of one's brother-in-law," Beatrice rebuked. "But as it is no great secret, I shall answer. Poor Nicholas has no money at all. His father, I believe, was a minister in India."

"I think there is something I am missing." Tommy shook his head, hopelessly befuddled. "Why didn't your father care about Nicholas's lack of finances when it seems he was open about his desire to increase his own fortune?"

"That's very simple. When Frances announced she wanted to marry Nicholas, father had our mother's money, and what he believed was a back up flow of money from Les. Of course, when our mother died, he became quite desperate. Especially when it was clear there would be no pot of gold from Les or his family."

"So he focused his attentions on my mother, believing she could convince me to part with money." It wasn't a question, it was the truth. Tommy was sure of that because he knew how much money his mother had asked him for the previous evening.

"She tried, didn't she?" Beatrice looked at him with sympathy.

"How do you know that?"

"Come now, Lord Northmoor, I've been incredibly honest with you." Beatrice considered him, her head tilted slightly to one side. "Credit me with a little intelligence. My father encouraged Helen to speak with you last night. I'm certain that was to ask for a ridiculously large sum of money."

How had the conversation turned so completely? He was supposed to be asking Beatrice questions so he could find out who had a good motive for killing the Marquess, but the woman was talking about his own family secrets.

Tommy didn't doubt that the answer to Beatrice's suggestion was clear on his face. Eventually, he replied. "It was an unseemly amount of money."

Beatrice looked away. "I doubt your mother would have returned from her honeymoon. She's had a very lucky escape."

"You believe your father would have killed Mother?" Tommy forced the question past his tight throat. The conversation had a very surreal feeling about it, but Beatrice's suggestion had the ring of truth about it.

"You asked earlier about Father's heir?"

Tommy nodded, unable to follow Beatrice's chain of thought. "Yes."

"Have you heard of Lady Adeline Cameron?"

Who hadn't? She was the current darling of the London social scene. "Of course."

"That's who Father really wanted to marry."

"But she's—"

"Yes." Beatrice interrupted. "Young enough to be his daughter. Younger than Frances and me, in fact."

"Would she have married him?"

"Are there any young girls who go through a London season and don't wish to marry a Duke, a Marquess, or an Earl?"

"I don't know," Tommy answered honestly.

"Ask your sisters if they'd rather marry an ordinary gentleman, or one with a title."

"This is rather a lot to take in."

Beatrice gave him a sympathetic smile. "You walked out here to find out if I hated my father enough to kill him, and I'm afraid all I've given you is the perfect motive for Harry to have killed my father."

"Did you do it?" Tommy asked quickly, desperate to find out something more before he ran back to the house to find his brother with renewed purpose. He'd tear every room apart if he had to. If Beatrice had told the police the information she had just shared with him, Harry was certain to be their primary suspect.

"Kill my father?" Beatrice peered over Tommy's shoulder in the direction of the house. "I believe the police detective is on his way across your lawn to speak to you."

"Oh, golly." Tommy pulled a hand through his hair.

"I didn't kill him. I had nothing to gain from his death, other than peace from his wicked tongue, of course."

Which was as good a motive as any, Tommy supposed.

"Northmoor!" Detective Sergeant Montgomery called. "Where is your brother? The Detective Inspector is waiting to interview him!"

~

*E*velyn found Frances, the Marquess's younger daughter, in the drawing room with Aunt Em.

"My dear," Aunt Em said. "You look positively worn out. Do sit down and have a rest from whatever it is that's making you so weary."

Evelyn smiled and longed to tell Aunt Em her concern was for Harry. As she left Jane Simmons in the library, she had heard Detective Inspector Andrews shouting forcefully at his junior detective that he must find Harry Christie immediately. She feared they would not solve the mystery before they found Harry and she hated to think what that may mean for Tommy's younger brother.

"I think the extra work planning the wedding has rather caught up with me."

"I would imagine finding my father's body this morning hasn't helped," Frances commented, her voice devoid of any emotion.

"No, it was very shocking."

"I have every confidence Lord and Lady Northmoor will uncover the dastardly perpetrator," Aunt Em said proudly. "They are extremely good sleuths. Much better than those who get paid to do the job."

"Have you spoken to the police?"

"Indeed." Aunt Em indicated Frances Lester. "Lady Frances and I were just discussing who could have done it."

Frances's lips twitched. "I told Lady Emily it could be almost anyone," Frances confided. "Father was a dreadful bully."

"Who is your chief suspect?" Evelyn asked as innocently as she could.

"The obvious one is your mother-in-law. Did you see how tightly Father was grasping her hand last night? Then he forced her to ask her own son for money. The humiliation would be enough to cause her to commit murder, I'm sure."

"The police suspect Harry," Aunt Em added. "Which is ridiculous. The boy is barely out of short trousers."

Evelyn hid an irreverent smile. Now wasn't the time to show amusement at Aunt Em's witty quips. "I don't think his young age is a barrier to murder. But I do agree, Harry simply can't have done it. He's such a sweet boy."

"Being sweet is no barrier to murder," Frances threw Evelyn's words back at her. "Everyone has a limit that, when reached, can explode in a show of anger."

That sounded rather personal. "Do you know of anyone who has lost their temper recently?"

"I do not."

The emphasis Frances put on the word 'I' intrigued Evelyn. "Then who has?"

"You should speak to my sister. She overheard something in the billiard room last night. Beatrice said there was the most frightful scene."

"Do you know who was involved?"

"My father, of course." Frances shrugged. "That should almost go without saying. He has ferocious rows with people wherever he goes."

"To whom was he speaking?"

"I don't know." Frances frowned. "Beatrice didn't say. She looked frightened and changed the subject when I started asking questions."

Evelyn hoped Tommy had gleaned the information from his talk with Beatrice. It was possible whoever was arguing with the Marquess was also the murderer. Or was that assumption too great a leap? Frances said that almost anyone could have a reason to kill her father. It didn't necessarily follow that a blazing argument would precede murder.

"I don't suppose you know who your father's heir is?"

"Do you think whoever it is killed the Marquess?" Aunt Em raised an eyebrow. "I shouldn't imagine he was worth killing, except for his title."

"Well, really," Frances spluttered.

"I apologise if I've offended you, Lady Frances," Em said placatingly. "But now really isn't the time to hide things that may be important in uncovering the person who killed your father. His finances are quite obviously in a terrible state."

"How would you know such a thing?" Evelyn asked.

"Well, that's simple." Aunt Em folded her hands in her lap, the very picture of a docile older lady. Only the spark of light in her faded blue eyes showed she was one of the sharpest people Evelyn had ever met. "The Marquess wouldn't have decided to marry Helen if he had a bean to his name."

"You seem to know a lot about our family affairs," Frances said stiffly.

"I know your father is keen on Lady Adeline Cameron." Aunt Em leaned forward. "But, of course, she doesn't have a fortune the size of the Christie one behind her."

Evelyn was appalled at Aunt Em's outspokenness, but Frances Lester simply laughed. "Is there anything you don't know?"

Em smiled a little smugly. "I like to know what is going on around my family."

"Quite right too," Frances said approvingly. "Poor Lady Northmoor looks rather shocked."

It all seemed so very wrong, that marriages were being spoken of as though they were business transactions. A thought occurred to her. "I don't suppose Tommy would have been allowed to marry me had he been Lord Northmoor before we met."

"Don't be silly, my dear." Aunt Em patted Evelyn's hand. "The Christie fortune has always been very secure. If it was in trouble, Eddie would never have been allowed to marry that awfully vain creature he tied himself to."

Lillian Christie was the widow of Tommy's cousin, Eddie.

It was an understatement to suggest she had not been popular when she lived at Hessleham Hall.

"Can we get back to your father's heir?" Evelyn asked Frances, hoping to move the conversation away from family finances. It made her very uncomfortable and all too well aware that everything she had was because of Tommy's inheritance. She had brought nothing to the marriage except for herself, and it seemed that being useful in doing something so simple as producing an heir was beyond her capabilities.

"I can't help you," Frances said dismissively. "I do not know who it could be. It wasn't the sort of thing that Father would ever discuss with either Beatrice or me, given we are only girls."

"I appreciate Aunt Em doesn't think your father could have been killed for his inheritance, but people have been killed for a lot less. Who will know the identity of the heir?"

"I suppose the family solicitor may know." Frances looked at Aunt Em. "Unless there's something Lady Emily can share with us. She does seem to be very well informed."

"Your father had two younger brothers. The brother closest in age to your father would be the heir presumptive."

Frances screwed up her face in thought. "I think one brother is dead. The other, I believe, went off to fight in the Boer War and never came home, though I don't think he died."

Evelyn recalled that Helen's godfather, Sir Richard Carlisle had fought in the Boer War. Was it possible he knew of the Marquess's brother? Or, at least, perhaps he had a contact from his days in the Army that he could telephone for information. She made a mental note to discuss that with Tommy.

Her list was growing. She also needed to speak to him about Constance and Alexander Ryder, and also a cottage for Nora and Albert. No wonder Aunt Em thought she looked

harried, her mind was overloaded with things she needed
to do.

She had grown to accept her life at Hessleham Hall and
even, on occasion, enjoy it, but at that moment she felt thoroughly unprepared and overwhelmed with her responsi-
bilities.

~

*T*ommy hurried toward the stables. He'd racked his
brains to think of somewhere an extremely inebri-
ated young man may go to sleep off his overindulgence.
Perhaps if Harry had left the house for some fresh air, he had
ended up at the stables? He knew Partridge had already
searched, but there was no harm in looking again.

Leslie Dawson, Beatrice's husband, looked around as
Tommy rushed into the stable block and peered into each
stall. Slowly, Tommy turned back to the other man. "What is
that you have there?"

The tool in Leslie's hand clattered onto the table in the
horse box they kept empty for the local farrier to come and do
his work. "I don't know, Lord Northmoor. Do excuse me, I
was bored in the house, and came for a look around. I hope
you don't mind."

"Of course not," Tommy said cautiously, not wanting to
move closer to the other man until he was certain Leslie
wasn't a threat. "Hopefully the police will finish their investigations soon and allow people to return to their homes."

"I wonder for how long Yorkville Manor will remain our
home," Les said pensively.

"I was speaking about that with your wife earlier. Perhaps
the new owner, whoever he may be, will be happy for you to
go on living there."

"Oh I shouldn't think either of us would want that. We
only stayed because Beatrice didn't want to leave her mother.

65

Even after her death, she felt close to her in her family home. Now I think it would be best if Beatrice, the children, and I found somewhere of our own to live. In fact, I will insist upon it."

"The Marquess was a difficult man to live with, I understand?"

"Impossible," Les said with feeling. "A quite frightful individual."

"I heard how he spoke to your wife last night."

Les's gaze snapped angrily to Tommy's. "I expect you think I should've defended my wife against the tyrant?"

Tommy didn't see any point in lying. "I wouldn't let anyone speak to my wife in that manner. In fact, I challenged the Marquess about the way he spoke about my mother."

"Don't you see that you have the power to do that?" Les said, a pleading note in his voice. His momentary anger now dissipated as quickly as it had begun.

"How so?"

"You see yourself as the Marquess's equal."

"You did not?"

Les barked out a laugh. "Certainly not. He tolerated me while he thought I may be useful as a source of income for him when he needed it. Once he knew my money was all tied tightly in our family trust, I was of no use to him. After being treated as an inferior specimen for so long, one rather starts to believe it."

Tommy couldn't imagine anyone making him feel so cowed, but then he had never had to live with a man as ghastly as the Marquess. Perhaps he should have more sympathy for his mother, rather than the blazing anger he felt every time he thought of his mother allowing the Marquess to squeeze her hand so harshly or following his direction and asking Tommy for a sum of money that made his eyes water.

As awful as those things were, his real fury was reserved for the way his mother was so desperate to marry the

Marquess, she was prepared to transfer responsibility for her children onto Tommy. He would be only too happy to care for his sisters and brother, that wasn't the problem, it was the callous way his mother intended to cast them to one side for a man.

"I have to ask." Tommy walked closer to Les now there did not seem to be an imminent threat from the other man. "Do you know who could have killed the Marquess?"

"I can't imagine there is a motiveless person here in the house." Les shook his head. "As I've said, he was a most unlikeable fellow."

Tommy picked up the tool that had dropped from Les's hand as he came into the stables. "Used for cutting out excess sole and frog in a horse's shoe. Not that I know what that means, it's just what the farrier tells me. He likes to talk while he's shoeing the horses."

"I was just looking," Les said again, this time a little more defensively. "I don't know why. I don't particularly like horses, so I don't even know why I came in here."

"No harm done," Tommy assured Les. "I'm glad I saw you looking at those tools when I came in. I'd never really thought about it before but having such things easily accessible probably isn't such a good idea when children visit regularly."

"Surely any children that visit Hessleham Hall are adequately supervised?" Les frowned, sounding more like Andrew at that moment than he had the rest of their conversation. "It's not as if they would be rooting around the stables by themselves, is it?"

That was probably true, but Tommy couldn't help the shiver that ran down his spine when he looked at the farrier's knife. Evelyn had described the one that killed Andrew as being rather old and worn looking. Was it possible the farrier had another, similar knife, and that one was the murder weapon?

He might not have known the murder was going to take place, but he couldn't help a feeling of responsibility if the murderer had access to a weapon because Tommy had such things lying around in his stables. It was something he needed to discuss with Detective Inspector Andrews.

"I don't suppose you've seen my brother while you've been exploring?" Tommy pulled a hand through his hair. He didn't want to draw attention to the fact Harry was missing, but time was running out.

"Goodness me," Les stepped backward, shock evident in his face. "You don't think he's been done in too?"

Tommy didn't think that. At least, he hadn't until Les suggested it. He'd been more worried Harry was somehow involved in Andrew's death. But Les did have a point. What if Harry was a victim?

"Excuse me," Tommy said as he stumbled past Les. "I really must find my brother."

# CHAPTER 6

"Oh, Mr Lester," Evelyn injected a note of what she hoped sounded like surprise as she walked into the billiard room—she'd been looking for the man for over half an hour. Hessleham Hall contained entirely too many rooms when one wanted to find someone quickly. "Do excuse me."

"Lady Northmoor." Nicholas Lester got to his feet and nodded politely in her direction.

"I don't suppose you have seen my husband's cigars?"

"I'm afraid not," Nicholas said. "Though I haven't looked, of course. I've only been here for a couple of minutes."

He sat back in one of the comfortable chairs. Evelyn made a show of looking around a few of the side tables before moving over to a large display cabinet to Nicholas's left. She lifted the body of the elephant statue and peered inside.

"Lady Northmoor, pardon me, but are you looking for Lord Northmoor's cigars because your husband has hidden them from you or because you want to give them to him?"

His words were delivered with a smile and Evelyn warmed to the man. "I simply wanted to check how many are left."

"That's very kind of you," Nicholas said. "What a very admirable wife you are."

Evelyn chuckled, hating the lies that she believed were necessary to strike up a conversation with Nicholas. "I must admit I usually leave such tasks to the staff, but Tommy does enjoy a smoke when he is thinking about things. He's very worried about his brother, Harry. I don't suppose you have seen him, have you?"

"I'm afraid not." Nicholas moved over to stand next to Evelyn and examined the statue. "What a beautiful piece of work."

"It is rather fine," Evelyn agreed, though she had never given the ornament a second thought. It was simply one of many things that had been in the house for goodness only knew how long. "I think I'd rather like to see an elephant in real life."

"They are magnificent creatures," Nicholas said.

"Oh, you've seen one? You lucky thing."

Nicholas laughed. "Practically every day when I was a boy in India."

"Lord Northmoor is keen for us to take a holiday." Evelyn replaced the top of the elephant. "Perhaps I should suggest India, I hear it is a wonderful country."

"Yes." Nicholas seemed to be lost in his own memories for a few moments. "I was very happy there. Sometimes..."

"Yes?" Evelyn pressed.

He smiled wryly. "Sometimes I wish I had never left."

"England cannot compare?"

"They each have their different qualities," Nicholas said. "Life was certainly much simpler in India."

"A murdered father-in-law does rather cause a lot of complications."

"I shan't miss him." Nicholas glanced at Evelyn. "I expect that sounds shocking to you, Lady Northmoor?"

"It seems to be universally accepted that he wasn't a very

pleasant man," she said. "As for shocking me, honesty very rarely does that."

"He was extremely brutish towards poor Frances," Nicholas admitted.

"She was in the drawing room with Lady Emily earlier," Evelyn said. "She wasn't at all emotional at the passing of her father."

"None of us are."

Evelyn decided to push on while Nicholas was talking so openly with her and ask the question that she really wanted an answer to. "Do you know who the Marquess's heir is?"

"Yes," Nicholas said, his voice low. "But I fear if that information were to become common knowledge, the fellow would be the prime suspect."

"I expect that is true. Whoever he is, that man must have hidden his identity for many years."

"I suppose so." Nicholas turned to look out of the window.

Evelyn waited a moment, but when it was apparent he wasn't going to say anything else, she spoke again. "For example, one would expect the heir's surname to be Parsons. If, perhaps, he had changed it to something else it would allow him a degree of anonymity."

"Yes, it would. For a limited period of time." Nicholas appraised her and a prickle of apprehension shivered its way down Evelyn's spine. She liked the man, but that didn't mean he wasn't the missing heir, or that he hadn't killed Andrew.

"I'm sure the police are checking the identity of all the guests for someone who may be either the Marquess's younger brother, or perhaps another male relation."

"As I said, anonymity may only last for a short space of time."

"Do you not think that it would be easier for that person, should he be here in the house, to let himself be known before the police uncover the fact?" Evelyn asked. "If he waits, he surely looks more guilty."

"The police suspect your brother-in-law. I understand he is missing?"

Despite the warm day, Evelyn shivered. "Harry would not kill anyone."

She nearly repeated the words she'd spoken to Nicholas's wife, Frances, suggesting that Harry was a sweet boy. Being sweet did not mean a man could not be angered enough to take someone else's life. Conversely, it did not mean that being the heir to an old and established title and estate meant a man would kill to gain those things.

"None of us know what we may be capable of until we are tested." Nicholas spoke in the same low, neutral tone he'd used throughout their conversation, but Evelyn now sensed an inner strength underneath the man's geniality that made her feel decidedly uneasy.

"Did you kill him?"

Nicholas paused long enough to blink before answering. "I did not."

"Do you know who did?"

"I'm afraid I can't help you any further, Lady Northmoor." Nicholas Lester got to his feet. "I do hope you find your husband's cigars. I have a feeling he may need them."

Now what did that mean? Evelyn couldn't press him any further. Nicholas gave a polite little bow and exited the room leaving her both certain he was the missing heir and wondering how she could prove it. And, even if she could, would that mean the police would transfer their suspicions on to Nicholas Lester or still hold Harry at the top of their list?

∾

"Mother!" Tommy shook his mother's arm gently. When she didn't respond, he used a little more force and raised his voice. "Mother!"

"Whaaaat?" She looked up at him groggily. "Tommy?"

"I'm sorry to wake you, Mother, but we still can't find Harry."

Helen Christie struggled to sit upright in bed. Her face was creased where she'd laid on her bedding. How could she have gone back to sleep after finding out her fiancé was dead?

"Harry?" She repeated, confusion settling over her features.

The limit of his patience was reached. "Harry. Your youngest son."

"What about him?"

Tommy stalked to the window and forced himself to take deep breaths and attempt to calm down. "He is missing."

"Didn't you tell me that earlier?" Her voice was hesitant, unsure, and husky with sleep.

"I did." Tommy whirled around. "Which is why finding you in bed is such a surprise to me."

"The sleeping draught," Helen said. "It must still be affecting me."

Tommy sighed. "Mother, if you look at the clock, you will see that now is about the time your wedding should have been taking place. You cannot expect me to believe that if that event were still going ahead, you would be lying in your bed."

She put a hand up to her head and rested it across her forehead. "It's the strain of it all, Tommy. My nerves have been very badly affected."

"Harry is missing, and the police suspect him of killing Andrew." Tommy spoke gently, but his words echoed around the room with their quiet ferocity. "Are you hearing what I am telling you?"

"Well, that's ludicrous."

"Quite," Tommy agreed. "Now, what are you going to do about it?"

"Me?" Helen grabbed her wrap from the chair next to the bed, fastened it, then sat back heavily. The squeak of the bedsprings scraped on Tommy's nerves. How could she be so complacent, so uncaring? Why had he been so blind to her true nature before this weekend? "What are you going to do about it? You're the one with the influence."

"I can't influence the police, Mother."

"I don't think I like your tone." Helen reached over to the bell pull and yanked it. "Andrew—"

"Andrew was a bully," Tommy interrupted. "I can't find anyone who has a single pleasant thing to say about him."

"They didn't know him like I do," Helen said sulkily. "He could be very sweet when the mood struck."

"Whose idea was it that you get married here?" Tommy changed the subject quickly. "It seems an odd place to choose. Didn't Andrew want to get married in his own home?"

Helen looked away. "We thought it would be nice for my side of the family to have the wedding somewhere they felt comfortable."

Tommy didn't believe that for a moment. He was convinced it was because it was because the financial burden for the wedding fell squarely upon his shoulders. "Is it possible Andrew was marrying you because of my money?"

"Thomas!" Helen squeaked. "What a dreadful thing to say about your own mother. Is it impossible to believe that he wanted to marry me because I'm a very attractive woman for my age?"

"It has been suggested to me you were happy to marry Andrew so you could enjoy the title of Marchioness. Would it therefore be so absurd to think that Andrew had his own reasons for marrying you?"

"You must tell me immediately who said such a vile thing."

"Is it true?"

Helen stared at Tommy as though she was only just seeing him for the first time. "Why are you being like this?"

"I'm trying to find out who killed Andrew so the police do not arrest Harry. I'm sorry if you don't like my questions, Mother, but I feel that I must ask them."

"Will they arrest Harry when he is found?"

"Almost certainly."

Helen pleated the edge of her bedspread with her fingers. "I was rather enthralled with the idea of being a Marchioness."

"And Andrew?" Tommy pressed.

"He did talk about money much more than I thought was polite."

There was something missing in the way Helen spoke about her fiancé, even though her reaction to his death earlier that morning had seemed genuine enough. "Did you love him?"

"Well," Helen spluttered. "Is that a question you should be asking your mother?"

"Did you?"

"Of course." Helen looked relieved as there was a knock at her bedroom door. "Enter."

One of the young maids came into the room and looked between Helen and Tommy. "You rang, Mrs Christie?"

"I would like a tea tray brought up immediately." Helen got to her feet and moved over to sit in a chair next to the fire-place. "Ensure it is piping hot, I detest cold tea. And have someone come and light the fire in my room. It's uncommonly cold in here."

"Yes, Mrs Christie." The girl bobbed her knee. "I will see to it immediately."

Tommy pulled open the curtains in his mother's room and

allowed the brilliant sunlight to fill the room. "It's the middle of August."

"Tommy, really." Helen held up a hand to shade her eyes. "Don't you know how bad the sun is for delicate skin like mine? Do you want a mother ravaged by wrinkles, like an old leather horse saddle?"

He wanted a mother who cared where her youngest son was at that very moment. It didn't particularly bother him what she looked like. "Did you kill Andrew?"

"Now you've gone too far!" Helen shouted. "Your insolence is not only unbecoming of a man of your stature, but it's an embarrassingly disrespectful way to speak to your mother."

"Did you not hear how Andrew spoke to his children?"

"He found the girls tiresome."

Tommy longed to tell Helen that he found her behaviour worse than tiresome, but she was right about one thing—he'd probably already gone too far. "He was cruel."

"They were frumpy and boring, just like their mother."

"I felt sorry for you last night," Tommy said. "It appeared that you were going to marry a man who was a bit of a brute. But now I see his cruelty has rubbed off on you. I am truly ashamed of your behaviour."

He hurried over to the door. Why had he wasted his time finding out if his mother knew where Harry may be instead of just carrying on his search for his brother? He'd squandered valuable minutes with a woman who clearly cared about nothing but herself.

$\sim$

*E*velyn made her way wearily up to the nursery floor. The day had been exhausting already, and it was barely lunchtime. She had asked the housekeeper, Mrs Chapman, to set out a buffet luncheon in the cool dining room so people could eat as and when they pleased. She was too tired to care whether her guests thought her plan horribly unconventional. It hadn't been a very ordinary day.

She pushed open the door to the nursery and was pleased to see Josephine was awake. The baby belonged to Tommy's cousin, Madeleine, and was born earlier that year in the Christie home in Belgrave Square, London.

"Good day, Nanny."

"Oh, Lady Northmoor," Elsie Warren looked away from the window and toward Evelyn. "I wasn't sure we would see you up here today."

"May I?" Evelyn held out her arms, and Elsie placed Josephine in her embrace. Evelyn closed her eyes as she breathed in the sweet baby scent. "I wouldn't miss spending time with this sweet child for anything."

"Are you and Lord Northmoor sleuthing again?"

"Yes, we must. Have you heard that Lord Northmoor's brother is missing?"

"Everyone has been looking for him," Elsie said. "He's such a handsome man."

Evelyn glanced at Elsie and raised an eyebrow. The younger woman coloured. "You haven't seen Master Harry?"

"I haven't," Elsie confirmed. "I do beg your pardon for speaking out of turn."

"You must try harder not to speak in haste," Evelyn said. "I would hate for Lord Northmoor to hear you speaking in such a way about his brother."

"Yes, My Lady." Elsie looked down. "I'm very sorry."

Evelyn smiled at the baby and was delighted to receive one in return. "You may go down to the kitchen to arrange Miss Josephine's lunch."

Elsie left the room and Evelyn considered the uncharacteristically critical way she'd spoken to the young woman who worked on the nursery floor. Elsie had helped Evelyn's sister, Milly, earlier that year when she had given birth to twins.

Milly had only good things to say about Elsie. However, the nanny's comments about Harry had concerned Evelyn. Probably because the young woman had been involved with a married villager the previous year.

Evelyn talked to the baby and drank in her innocence. Was it possible that she'd been around evil so many times that she saw it everywhere? Elsie had made a mistake in her past, but it wasn't fair that Evelyn should judge her for it now. After all, if Nora had made a comment about Harry's good looks, she wouldn't feel as defensive.

"Good afternoon, Evelyn." Madeleine walked into the room and, as always, Evelyn was impressed by the young woman's calm demeanour and cool, blonde beauty. She remembered a time when she was composed. Now it seemed she was forever worrying about things over which she had absolutely no control.

"How are you?"

"Never mind how I am," Madeleine retorted. "How are you? What a terrible thing to happen and after all your hard work too."

"I am tired," Evelyn said honestly, then wished she hadn't been quite so outspoken when Madeleine turned anxious eyes to her.

"Oh, you poor darling, you must let us all help more."

"You have the baby. She is more important than organising weddings or other such things."

"You and Tommy have employed a full-time nanny. Josephine also has a doting aunt, a grandmother who spends hours with her, as well as you, David, and me."

"She is rather lucky, isn't she?" Evelyn laughed as Josephine grabbed one of her fingers in her chubby fist.

"She is the luckiest little girl in the world," Madeleine confirmed. "Despite how difficult things were for her when she was born. I was so very afraid."

"And now you both have David, who adores both of you."

"I can't help feeling a little faithless. Poor Georges. But I did love him so."

Georges was Josephine's father. He had been killed at their London home earlier that year. "I didn't know him, but I'm certain he would want you and Josephine to be well cared for. I know David will do that."

"David is wonderful." Madeleine sighed. "I loved Georges very much, but now it feels like such an immature emotion compared to my feelings for David."

"He's a very special man."

"Did Tommy tell you that David asked if we could marry this weekend?"

"He did not! Goodness, how exciting."

"We would need to get a Special Licence which Alexander has said he can arrange for us."

Evelyn thought about the ramifications of allowing the wedding to go ahead. Although none of the Marquess's family seemed to care about him, it would still be in very poor form if she and Tommy allowed a wedding to go ahead at the house while they were still in residence. "I shall find a way to ask Lady Beatrice. She must agree before we can allow it to go ahead."

"Of course. I believe Tommy told David he would ensure neither his mother nor the police objected." Madeleine gazed at her daughter. The love in the young woman's eyes made Evelyn's stomach squeeze painfully. "Sometimes it's hard to think of other people's feelings when you're so desperately in love."

"I remember how that feels." Evelyn smiled at Madeleine. "When Tommy and I were first together, it was as though no one in the world existed but the two of us."

"You still look at each other in that way now." Madeleine

sighed wistfully. "What I see in your marriage is what I want for me and David."

"I think Elise and Hugh are the same way, aren't they?"

"Poor Hugh." Madeleine's look of bliss turned to concern. "His father has left him quite penniless, though Elise doesn't care one bit about that. She would marry Hugh regardless."

"Tommy would certainly help. He wouldn't send Elise into the marriage without a sizeable dowry."

"Oh we couldn't allow him to do that." Madeleine shook her head decisively. "You've both already done so much for us."

"We are your family," Evelyn said gently. "Hessleham Hall is a home for all of the Christie family, not just those who inherited the house and the land. Besides, I should like to see you tell Tommy he can't do something he has set his heart on doing. He can be incredibly stubborn."

"She's right," a male voice sounded behind the two women.

"Where have you been?" Evelyn cried as she turned around to see a dishevelled Harry standing in the doorway.

He tried to tame his hair, which was sticking up in all directions. "Have I missed that beastly wedding? I do hope I have."

"You've missed more than that," Evelyn said tartly. "But where have you been?"

Harry jerked a thumb in the direction of the corridor. "In my old room. Forgot I'm a grown up now and don't belong on the nursery floor."

"I think the amount of wine and brandy you had may have contributed to that forgetfulness."

"Don't." Harry held up a hand. "I don't think I can ever look at a decanter again without feeling desperately ill."

Evelyn got to her feet, handed the baby to her mother, and pulled on the bell pull in the corner of the room. She then gave it an extra tug. Her staff were aware that if two bells sounded in swift succession, they were needed immediately.

"We need to get you sobered up," she said urgently.

"What's the rush?" Harry asked lazily. "I don't care one jot if I miss the wedding."

"The wedding is off," Evelyn replied sharply. "The Marquess has been killed."

"He's dead?" The remaining colour leeched from Harry's face.

"Stabbed," Evelyn confirmed. "And your disappearance means you are the police's primary suspect."

"Me? I was passed out dead drunk."

"Yes, you." Footsteps sounded in the corridor. "Good, that sounds like one of the maids. I shall order strong coffee and we'll have you ship-shape before the police take you away for questioning."

"I'm afraid there's no time for that, Lady Northmoor." Detective Inspector Andrews stood glaring at her from the door. "You're coming with me, young man."

"But Detective." Evelyn moved to stand in front of Harry. "Can't you see the state of him? He was exceedingly drunk last night. He wasn't in any fit state to murder anyone."

"I only have your word for that, Lady Northmoor, and I am afraid it is simply not enough." He beckoned someone behind him, and a uniformed officer moved forward holding out handcuffs.

Polly pushed her way past the police and hurried into the room, panting. "Lady Northmoor?"

"I rang for coffee." Evelyn glanced at Harry's stricken face. "But please fetch Lord Northmoor. Immediately."

"Yes, My Lady."

Polly hurried off and Detective Inspector Andrews looked at Evelyn, his expression softened. "Lord Northmoor cannot stop me from arresting his brother."

"No," Evelyn agreed sadly. Tears stung her eyes, but she

refused to show weakness in front of Harry. He needed her to be strong and in control. "But surely you will allow Lord Northmoor a moment to speak with his brother before you take him away?"

"Out of courtesy to you both, and because of the assistance you have given in other cases, I will." He raised a hand and pointed at Harry. "But that young man has a lot of explaining to do. I'm certain neither you nor Lord Northmoor are aware he was overheard threatening the Marquess of York, are you?"

Evelyn looked at Harry and was about to ask him if the allegation was true, but the young man dropped his head into his hands. That was all the answer she needed.

"It's true," Harry muttered. "I did say I'd see him dead before he married my mother."

# CHAPTER 7

*T*ommy sat on the edge of the bed, his head held despondently in his hands. "I've failed my brother."

Evelyn sat next to him and rested a hand on his thigh. "You have failed no one, my love."

He looked up at her lovely face, but it didn't calm the frantic beating of his heart or the overwhelming emotions swirling through his body. "How can you say that? He's in handcuffs, in a police car, and on the way to York to be interrogated by detectives. Harry is not equipped for this. You saw how he was in the nursery, he practically admitted to killing Andrew."

"He admitted to threatening Andrew. It's not at all the same thing."

"It is to the police. All he has done is vindicate their decision that he was the primary suspect. The silly little fool."

"He's a young boy," Evelyn said softly, "who was afraid, probably had a horrific hangover, and was simply telling the truth."

Tommy got to his feet and stalked over to the window.

"What I'd like to know is who told the police they heard Harry threatening Andrew?"

"Why?" Evelyn asked in that same gentle voice. He knew she was trying to calm him down, but it infuriated him. Why wasn't she as outraged as he was? It was quite obvious his baby brother would not have driven a knife into Andrew's stomach—no matter how much he hated the man.

"Whoever told the police that has practically hung the noose around Harry's neck."

"Darling." Evelyn walked over to him and wrapped her arms around his waist. Ordinarily he would've turned into her embrace, but Tommy held himself stiffly as he continued to stare out of the window. "Whoever it was simply told the truth about what they overheard. Not everyone in this house has loyalty to this family, or Harry in particular."

He didn't want to say the words, but he forced them past his tight throat. "Do you think my mother could've snitched on Harry?"

"It could have been anyone," Evelyn said pragmatically. "But really, it doesn't matter. It's the truth and finding out who repeated Harry's accusation will not help us uncover the murderer."

"It is, if the killer repeated what he heard to divert attention from himself."

"You should hear what I learned from Nicholas Lester. I believe him to be the missing heir. If the police knew his identity, he would also be a suspect, but he's keeping quiet."

He turned to face her then, his anger at the person who repeated Harry's drunken threat forgotten for the moment. "Nicholas Lester? Really?"

"He didn't actually admit it, but he said enough to make me believe he is Andrew's heir. But of more interest is the fact he stated the police may struggle to prove the heir's identity and finally, he said it was impossible to know how far a person may go until they were in a sticky situation."

"What did he say that made you think it's him?"

"We were talking about India. He said he spent his childhood there."

Tommy raised an eyebrow. "That's very flimsy, Evelyn. I'm sure lots of people were born in India."

"We should take steps to check the circumstances surrounding his birth." Evelyn shrugged. "How does one go about doing that?"

"I don't know. I imagine the India Office would have the records. Or, perhaps, they are kept in India."

"Who would know? Aunt Em, or perhaps Sir Richard?"

"Let's ask them both. If we can prove Nicholas is the missing heir, it may at least give the police another suspect to look at."

"You're thinking too emotionally, Tommy." Evelyn lifted a hand to rest on his cheek. "There's absolutely no evidence against Harry because he didn't do it. The police will simply have to find another suspect. It's up to us to offer as many suspects their way as we can."

"Okay." Tommy grabbed Evelyn's hand and led her back over to the bed. "I shall count off what we know on your hand."

"That's the spirit," Evelyn encouraged.

Tommy wiggled her thumb. "The police told me they believe Andrew died last night."

"So, someone killed him shortly after you spoke to him?"

"It seems so," Tommy said. "But that is simply confirmation of what we already suspected. I told Detective Inspector Andrews about the farrier's tools in the stable. He is going to check out the possibility that Andrew was killed with a farrier's knife."

"Which the killer took because he planned to kill Andrew. Or perhaps we've been looking at that the wrong way around, and the killer picked it up to protect himself."

"You think he may have been afraid of Andrew?"

"Everyone has said what an awful person he was. Maybe he took the knife with him because he was scared and used it in self-defence."

Tommy thought for a moment. "Yes, that's possible. But then that's another person who could come forward and get Harry off the hook."

"Going armed with a weapon and claiming self-defence is pretty hard to prove, I would imagine."

Tommy picked up Evelyn's forefinger. "We need to work out how the killer got hold of one of Mother's handkerchiefs."

"Or contemplate that, in fact, the person we're looking for had the hankies because they belonged to her."

"Does it make me an awful person that it's so much easier to believe my mother killed Andrew than Harry?"

Evelyn raised their joined hands and brushed a kiss across Tommy's knuckles. "Not at all. It would make sense. Why would Harry have one of his mother's hankies in his pocket?"

"Why would anyone?"

"Indeed," Evelyn agreed. "Now, what is the next point we should consider?"

"Beatrice and Frances both have an excellent motive for killing their father. He was awful to both of them."

"Frances says Beatrice heard her father arguing with someone last night in the billiard room."

"Hmm," Tommy said. "Beatrice told me she heard Constance talking to Alexander in the same room. Perhaps Constance, or Alex, saw the person Andrew argued with."

Evelyn bit her lip. "I was going to tell you I'd heard whispers about Constance and Alexander."

"I intend to talk to her about it." Tommy hated the idea of his sister spending time with the new Earl of Chesden. Although he liked the Earl's brother David very much, the same couldn't be said for Alexander. Judging from the time they spent together in London, Alexander Ryder seemed to be a chip off the old block—and that was not a good thing.

"Point number four." Evelyn lowered her ring finger. "What do we know about Beatrice's husband?"

"Seems rather cowed by Andrew," Tommy replied. "But we cannot discount him just because he seems meek. Perhaps he had finally had enough of Andrew bullying both him and Beatrice?"

"I suppose the same can be said for Nicholas. Though he has the additional motive of being Andrew's missing heir."

"I'll see if I can find out who the family solicitor is. I don't expect they'll tell me anything, but perhaps they could telephone the police and let them know the identity of Andrew's heir."

"If he knows himself," Evelyn added.

"Beatrice was convinced her father was marrying Mother for money and then he intended to get rid of her and marry Lady Adeline Cameron and hope for an heir of his own."

"What a ghastly way to live one's life." Evelyn raised her eyes to Tommy's. "I do hope you won't throw me over for another woman if I cannot give you a male child."

"I forbid you to ever say such a thing ever again," Tommy said fiercely. "You are my wife. I married you for better, or for worse. I don't intend to ever let you go."

She ducked her head into his shoulder. "I'm sorry. It's just so difficult to hear about how some people choose to live their lives and not allow it to affect me."

"We've got a lot to work on," he said, abruptly changing the subject. After all, hadn't she just told him not to let his emotions interfere with their investigations? They must keep their minds on the mystery in front of them so they could solve it and secure Harry's release, sooner rather than later. "What did you think about Jane Simmons?"

"She said the same as everyone else. Andrew was a bully, and she didn't like the way he treated Frank."

"And yet Frank was his best man." Tommy ran a hand down Evelyn's back. "That suggests he was Andrew's closest friend, yet I didn't get that impression from Frank. He told me Andrew didn't really have any friends."

"So perhaps he preferred his best man to be someone he could bully and control?" Evelyn suggested.

"Frank intimated to me he really only suffered Andrew because he had a decent hunt."

"Gosh what a terrible epitaph." Evelyn's mouth curved into a smile. "Here lies the Marquess of York: he was an awful man, but he had an excellent hunt."

Tommy laughed. "You're right, that is terrible."

"What are we doing about David and Madeleine's request to marry?"

"I asked Detective Inspector Andrews before he left with Harry. He has no objections, so long as no one else comes to the house. I think Mother would say no if we gave her the choice. And, despite the animosity towards Andrew by everyone, I don't feel comfortable speaking with his family for their permission."

"You're right. We should concentrate on solving the murder and then perhaps when our guests have left and there's just family left, it can quietly go ahead."

"I'll ask Cook to save as much of the food as she can. Perhaps we can send any surplus that will waste to the village?" Evelyn's eyes turned sad once more. "Ordinarily I'd send it to the nearest children's home, but we won't be able to get it there, will we?"

"I'll speak to the police constable patrolling the front gate and see if he will allow George Hughes to meet Partridge to take anything Cook cannot keep."

George Hughes was the landlord of the village public house, the Dog and Duck, and a man both Tommy and Evelyn trusted to share the food with the rest of the village.

"One last thing," Evelyn said. "Is there any possibility of

us offering young Nora and her beau, Albert, a cottage on the grounds?"

"I shall speak to Partridge to make arrangements." Tommy nodded. "There are several empty cottages, as you know. I would be happy for Nora and Albert to start their lives together in one of them."

"Nora will be thrilled." Evelyn's eyes shone with joy. Tommy didn't need any reminders of why he loved his wife as much as he did—but here was an exceptional example. She cared as much about the people who worked in their home as she did her family.

"Albert has already asked for her hand?"

"He has. Cook looked nearly as excited as Nora."

"I have an idea," Tommy said.

"Which is?"

Tommy tapped the side of his nose. "That is for me to know, my darling, and you to find out when I am ready to tell you."

~

*E*velyn found Sir Richard Carlisle in the dining room and immediately felt sorry for him. By arranging a buffet style luncheon, she had inadvertently left him to eat alone.

"Sir Richard, forgive me," she said as she entered the room.

"Whatever for, Lady Northmoor?"

"You don't really know anyone, and my arrangements for luncheon have caused you to dine by yourself."

"My dear lady," Sir Richard said, his mouth twitching with amusement. His enormous moustache quivered as though it too was joining in the joke. "Unless I am at one of my clubs in London, I dine alone every day. Please do not upset yourself on my account."

"I'm afraid the death of the Marquess has ruined my carefully laid plans." Evelyn's hands flew to her cheeks, which burned in embarrassment. "Though, of course, any preparations I've made for the weekend are secondary to tragic events."

"Sit down." Sir Richard motioned to the seat next to his. "Please stop fretting. My understanding is that the Marquess was a thoroughly awful fellow and shall not be missed."

That was true, but Evelyn still felt guilty. She wanted people to enjoy their stay at Hessleham Hall, though she supposed no one was going to talk about her hospitality skills after this weekend. The conversation would all be about the murder.

"You're right." Evelyn took the seat he had indicated. "I worry too much. I think I'm just worried about letting Tommy down."

"The man adores you. Nothing you could possibly do, or say, would lead him to have a lesser opinion of you."

To her horror, tears stung her eyes. What on earth was wrong with her? Why was she allowing herself to get so overwrought? "You're very kind."

"Now," he said in a kindly voice. "I expect you want to find out what I know about the murder? Am I a suspect?"

Evelyn opened her mouth to automatically deny it, but Sir Richard raised an eyebrow and winked at her. "My understanding is that you hadn't met the Marquess, or his family, before this weekend. I'm not sure how you could be a suspect. What motive would you have?"

"Perhaps I have skeletons in my closet."

Sir Richard waggled his eyebrows and his moustache danced above his top lip. Evelyn couldn't help the giggle that escaped. "I can't imagine what secrets you would have that would cause you to murder a man you had never met."

"A man like me can't have secrets," he said. "I'm quite well known in London, you see. As you are aware, that town is full of frightful gossips. One only has to be seen leaving home wearing a new tie, and word has got around before you reach your destination."

"Tommy tells me you fought in the Boer War?"

"I did." Sir Richard teased the edge of his moustache. "A fellow sees the most terrible things during a war. Changes a man forever."

"Tell me about the Marquess," Evelyn said, changing the subject. Tommy didn't like to talk about his time serving in the Army, and it seemed that Sir Richard didn't either.

"All I knew about him was what I'd been told, by friends and by Helen."

"Were they favourable things?"

"Goodness, no." Sir Richard let out a laugh loud enough that it startled Evelyn. "My friends told me exactly what we've uncovered for ourselves this weekend. The man was a terrible bully. However, Helen's letters were full of praise for him, and they quite convinced me the two of them were entering a marriage based on mutual admiration and affection."

"Were you very surprised when you met him and saw for yourself what he was like?" Evelyn asked, wondering if it was possible Sir Richard was so fond of Helen that he killed Andrew to save her from marrying him.

"Not especially," Sir Richard answered. "I had heard of his character before I arrived. Dear Helen had written about the man she wanted to marry instead of the reality."

"It's been suggested she wanted to marry him solely to have the title of Marchioness. Does that sound like something Helen would do?"

"Sadly, yes." Sir Richard sighed regretfully. "I explained to Tommy only this morning that your mother-in-law is the type of woman who needs a powerful man to tell her what to do. I think she admired that side of Andrew."

"And his nasty, vindictive side?"

"I should imagine she simply pretended that didn't exist. It didn't suit her purpose, you see, so she dismissed it."

"Could she have killed the Marquess?" Evelyn didn't want to mention the handkerchief she had found. Whilst she may not think Sir Richard was a viable suspect, it still wasn't a good idea to let others know there was incriminating evidence.

"I should think it unlikely," he said. "But, to properly answer your question, she could have, yes. But then, we all could have, couldn't we?"

"There is no obvious time of death," Evelyn said carefully. "We simply know that he was alive after dinner. At some point, he left the drawing room and was not seen alive again. Because I did not find his body until this morning, he could have been killed at any time. Therefore, everyone in the house had an opportunity."

"Is it correct that young Harry has been arrested?"

"I'm afraid that it is."

"Helen must be distraught."

"Detective Inspector Andrews left his junior officer to speak with her."

"Perhaps I should sit with her? Is she in any state to be questioned after what she has gone through?" Sir Richard's face creased into an agitated frown. "The poor woman has lost her fiancé and now her son has been arrested. What is Tommy thinking to allow her to be alone at a time like this?"

Evelyn knew the answer to that: Tommy was doing everything he could to clear his brother's name. Harry was his primary focus, not his mother, who had shown herself to be extraordinarily self-centred. She didn't think their relationship would ever be the same when this weekend was over.

"The police…"

"The police can question Helen only with her permission. She isn't under arrest, so they cannot force her to talk. I'm sure the poor lady does not know that." Sir Richard got to his feet. "It's really too bad that Tommy has abandoned his mother in her time of need. I shall go offer my assistance."

Evelyn stayed in her chair long after Sir Richard had left the dining room. Sir Richard's reaction seemed rather excessive to her. Obviously, he had known Helen for many years, as he was her godfather. Did he think of her as a daughter, and that was the reason for his intense concern? Or was it possible that Helen's godfather had stronger feelings for her? If so, was it possible he had killed the Marquess to prevent the woman he loved from marrying another man?

~

Tommy met with his sisters in the billiard room. As soon as they sat down, he lit a cigar. He watched as the smoke he blew out drifted around the room before streaming through the open French doors and beyond.

Constance wrinkled her nose. "They are dreadfully smelly, Tommy."

"It helps me think," he retorted. "I must find a way to expose the actual murderer and secure Harry's freedom."

"Did he really threaten the Marquess?"

"I'm afraid so," Tommy confirmed. "I don't suppose either of you liked him very much either?"

"He was a horror," Constance said.

"Did Mother talk to you about what was to happen after the wedding?"

"Not a thing." Constance frowned at her brother. "Why?"

"She planned to sell the house in the village and live with Andrew on his estate."

"What was to happen to us?" Grace wondered.

"It seems Mother thought you two girls, and Harry, should come and live with me."

"She won't sell the house now, though, will she?"

Constance said crossly. "How could she have made such plans and never so much as discussed them with us?"

"You know why." Grace looked at their sister with sadness in her eyes. "It is because all she cares about is herself."

Tommy scrubbed a hand across his face. "If things were so bad, why didn't you tell me?"

His sisters stared at him before Constance eventually spoke. "She's always been like that. I think the only one who hasn't realised it before now is you."

"Have I been so busy with my life here I didn't see how bad things were for you all?"

"It's not as though she was cruel," Grace said in their mother's defence. "You're talking as though you left us in the workhouse or something equally grim."

"Shall you stay with her?"

"Absolutely not," Constance snapped. "I have no intention of staying with her now I know she was only too happy to leave us with no home when she married that awful man. May we come here, Tommy?"

"I should be incredibly pleased if you did." Tommy smiled at his younger sister. His expression then turned serious as he looked at Constance. "For one thing, it will allow me to keep an eye on you and monitor potentially unsuitable suitors."

"Oh, Tommy!" Constance cried. "You can't possibly be talking about the Earl of Chesden. He is positively dreamy!"

"Earlier this year he was madly in love with Elise," Tommy said drily. Now was not the time to temper his words. Not when his sister's heart may be at risk.

"Was he really?" Constance giggled. "He must like Christie girls very much."

"Doesn't that news bother you at all?"

"Tommy, you absolute darling." Constance laughed with carefree abandon. "I've known the fellow less than twenty-four hours. It's jolly flattering that an Earl is taking notice of little old me, but it's not as though there are many other young ladies for him to talk to here this weekend, is it?"

Tommy exhaled the breath he didn't realise he had been holding. It was a relief to know he didn't have to chase Alexander Ryder off, as well as solve a murder, deal with his mother, and arrange for his brother to be released from custody.

"I must ask you something else, Constance." Tommy watched his sister's reaction as he spoke. "Is it true that you went into the billiard room with the Earl of Chesden last night?"

"It is." Spots of colour appeared high on Constance's cheekbones, but she didn't look away from his penetrating gaze.

"May I ask what for?"

"Simply to talk, Tommy." Constance leaned forward, her voice earnest. "The drawing room was full of stuffy old people. We just wanted to talk."

"The proper place for unmarried young people to talk is in the drawing room where they are properly chaperoned," Tommy said as severely as he could. "I shall talk to the Earl of Chesden about the type of behaviour expected in my house."

"You're right." Constance looked down at her hands, her face flushed. "I'm sorry."

"Now, while you were in the billiard room talking," he went on in a gentler voice, "did you happen to discuss how desperately Mother wanted to have the title of Marchioness?"

Constance fidgeted but, to her credit, she looked back at Tommy. "Someone overheard our conversation?"

"Yes," Tommy confirmed. "Someone did. It's true, then?"

"Mother is awfully jealous of Evelyn. She was incredibly pleased when Andrew started courting her. All she could talk about was that she would be a Marchioness, and Evelyn only a Countess."

"Why would Mother be envious of my wife? I simply don't understand."

"If Father had lived, he would be the Earl of Northmoor, and she would be Lady Northmoor. She feels as though Evelyn has what should have been hers."

"But that's…"

"Yes, ridiculous, we know," Grace said.

"Do all women want to marry a chap with a title?"

"Yes, mostly." Constance grinned. "We firstly hope to fall madly in love, of course."

"Preferably with a prince," Grace said with a dreamy look on her face.

"Why?" He asked, genuinely perplexed.

"Parties, grand houses, foreign holidays." Constance shrugged, as though the answer was obvious.

"New dresses, all the finest things, and a brand new motor car." Grace's eyes shone with excitement as she spoke.

"Are all of those things really important to you girls?"

"Oh, yes," Constance said. "But only if you're in love."

Grace shuddered. "I couldn't marry a fellow because he had those things if I didn't love him. Imagine waking up every single day to Frederick Baron."

"Grace, don't be unkind. Frederick is a fine young man," Tommy admonished, though he could see his sister's point. Poor Frederick Baron had not been blessed with good looks.

"Now, Constance, this is important." Tommy waited until he was sure he had his sisters' full attention and they had both stopped dreaming about the material things they wanted in their lives. "Did you see anyone going in or out of the billiard room? Either as you and Alex were going in, or coming out?"

"No, I didn't even know there was someone there listening to our conversation."

"Are you sure you didn't see anyone? It could be crucial. You see, Lady Beatrice overheard an argument that night between her father and another man. She refuses to say who this other man is, but I think it's vitally important we know his identity."

Tommy saw Constance's face change the moment she remembered something. "I saw that Simmons fellow heading in that direction when Lord Chesden and I went back to the drawing room, but I couldn't say if he definitely went in there. Though he had his pipe in his hand, so I think that's why I assumed he was going to that room. To smoke."

"Thank you, Constance, that's very helpful."

He must talk to Frank Simmons immediately. Was he the man Beatrice heard arguing with her father shortly before his death? Or did he perhaps know the identity of that man?

# CHAPTER 8

*E*velyn found Jane Simmons in the library once more. She sat staring at nothing in particular, with a different book on her lap.

"What are you reading?"

"Oh, Lady Northmoor." Jane half rose as though she was going to stand up, then sat back down. The knuckles on the back of her hands were white where she gripped the book with an intensity that Evelyn found quite alarming. "How lovely to see you again. I have this new book. At least, it's new to me. I've never read it before."

She held up the cover so Evelyn could read it. "Ah, a detective story."

"I'm not as clever as you," Jane said as she chattered on, barely taking a breath in between her words. "I shan't be sleuthing. But it's a very entertaining read. Have you read it? I believe Agatha Christie is a new author. Goodness, do you think she's a relation? That would be simply superb wouldn't it?"

"I haven't read it." Evelyn took the seat opposite Jane. "Though it seems like something I would enjoy."

"Oh you must take it." Jane held the book out to Evelyn. "It's your book, after all. You simply must read it."

"You finish it first, Mrs Simmons," Evelyn said. "When you've read it, tell me what you think and if you feel you can recommend it to me, I shall read it then."

"Oh, I couldn't presume to recommend something to you, Lady Northmoor."

"I absolutely insist."

"It is really rather good. The owner of a grand old house is dead, she's recently married a younger man. And really, anyone could have killed her. Just like the poor Marquess of York."

"Then I shall look forward to reading it myself. Perhaps when the murder of the Marquess has been solved. Did you perhaps know the Marchioness?"

Jane clapped her hands and looked animated. "Oh, Clara, she was the sweetest of women. We were very good friends."

"Clara?"

"Oh yes, she was most determined that I address her by her given name. Not in front of others, of course. She wouldn't have dared allow that. The Marquess would have been furious. We knew better than to do anything that would cause his temper to flare." Jane looked at Evelyn, her dark brown eyes sad with memories of her friend. "He was quite unhinged when his anger took hold of him."

"Was he cruel to Clara?"

"Unspeakably," Jane confirmed. "She didn't confirm to me he was the cause of her taking to her bed when the girls were young. Not in so many words, that is. But it was quite clear it was his doing."

"What do you think he did to her?"

Jane looked away. "I couldn't possibly know for certain. It could have been an accident."

Evelyn wanted to press the other woman and find out the reason Clara Parsons had spent the last years of her life confined to her bed. But was it relevant? Could something that happened over twenty years ago have led to the Marquess's death that weekend?

"Can you tell me about it?"

"I'm not sure I should." A look of fear settled on Jane's face and she glanced around the room as though someone was about to jump out with a weapon and threaten her at any moment.

Evelyn got to her feet and walked over to the library door. She closed it firmly, then retook her seat. "It may help in uncovering the killer."

"That's just the thing," Jane whispered. "Don't you see?"

"I'm not sure that I do."

"Perhaps it's best if the murderer isn't caught."

Evelyn thought carefully, so she would frame her next words in a way that would calm Jane's worries and hopefully encourage her to tell Evelyn more about what she knew. "Do you mean if the murderer turns out to be someone that has suffered greatly because of the Marquess's wickedness?"

"Yes, that's it exactly. Clara was such a dear, sweet friend. It could even be me that killed her husband as an act of retribution for the years of torment she suffered." Jane laughed, a high shrill sound that reminded Evelyn of the screech of seagulls as they flew overhead.

In that moment, Jane looked a little mad, and Evelyn felt the tingle of fear raise the hairs on the back of her neck. "Will you tell me what you know?"

Jane's face lost its manic look, and she leaned forward. "It was a riding accident. At least, that's how the Marquess explained it to everyone. Clara wasn't a good rider. If only I had stayed with her that day, but I enjoy riding so very much. We don't have horses at home, Frank and I, so if we are invited anywhere for a hunt, we always go. Of course, we had horses when I was a little girl. But that was so long ago now."

Evelyn didn't want to interrupt Jane's reminisces, but she

was desperate to hear the secret the other woman was slowly revealing. If only Jane didn't take so very long to get to the point! "Do you think the incident wouldn't have happened if you'd stayed with Clara?"

"He wouldn't have struck her if I were there," Jane said adamantly.

"He hit her? The Marquess attacked Clara?"

"No one knows exactly what happened except the two of them, and neither of them is here now to tell us. Clara would never explain to me properly. She came close a couple of times, but her tears stopped her from finishing the story. She was riding near the back of the group. The Marquess circled round to her and said she was embarrassing him with her poor horsemanship. She says he used his whip on her horse's flank and the shock of the strike caused the horse to rear."

"She fell off?" Evelyn breathed. "But you said he struck Clara, not the horse."

"Yes." Jane's eyes turned nearly black as her visage contorted into pure rage. "Clara had angry red marks on her hands after the accident. The only way that could have happened is if she too had been hit by a whip."

Evelyn wanted to shake her head and deny what Jane was saying because the conclusion she drew from her words was so terrible. "You think he whipped Clara's hands while she was desperately trying not to fall off the horse?"

"Maybe he hit her first." Jane lifted a shoulder. "I don't know, and Clara would never say. But her hands would not have been marked like that from falling off her horse. Whip marks are very distinctive."

"Clara wasn't able to walk after that?"

"No." Jane looked proudly back at Evelyn. "I was the only person Clara allowed to visit her in her bedroom. I was her very best friend, but still she wouldn't tell me the exact truth of what happened that day."

"She still protected the Marquess despite what he had done?"

Jane breathed in deeply through her nose. "I believe so."

The other woman was back to her usual demeanour—a little jittery with a mild, slightly vacant expression, but Evelyn couldn't help but think she'd seen parts of Jane that she kept well hidden. It made no sense that Jane had waited over twenty years before exacting her own form of revenge against the Marquess, but it wasn't a motive that should be discounted.

~

Malton pointed Tommy in the direction of the stream that ran along the edge of the lawn. Although he couldn't see Frank Simmons from the house, he had no reason to doubt Malton's assurances that was where he would be found. There wasn't a single thing that happened in the house that Malton did not know about.

As Tommy got nearer to the stream, he saw Frank sitting on a bench under a canopy of trees that gave welcome shade from the blistering sun.

"Northmoor," Frank greeted him. "It's unseasonably warm today, isn't it?"

"Hottest day I've known in years."

Frank looked longingly at the stream. "Makes a man wish he was a youngster again so he could take off his shoes and socks, roll up his trousers and paddle in the cool water."

Tommy looked up at the house, then back to Frank. "I'm willing to pretend and say no more about it if you are."

Frank laughed, a deep rumbling sound that erupted from his chest. "I say, shall we really?"

"Yes, let's."

The two men untied their shoes, then stuffed their socks inside, and worked on rolling up their trouser legs.

"Oh, this is simply delightful," Frank said in delight as he stood in the cool water. "If the Marquess could see us now!"

"What would he say?"

"He would be completely outraged." Frank grinned at Tommy before his face clouded over. "Then he'd probably threaten to tell everyone unless you paid for his silence."

"Blackmail?" Tommy asked sharply. Could there be a more sinister reason for murder?

"Yes." Frank looked down at the river flowing over his toes, regret for his hastily spoken words clear.

"Did he do that often?"

"Often enough."

"To you?"

"To everyone."

Tommy's mind raced. If the Marquess couldn't access Les's money because it was tied up in a trust, had he tried blackmailing his son-in-law out of it? If Andrew were that type of man, it seemed likely there were other people who had paid for his silence.

"I wish you had told me this earlier."

"No one wants to say something that could lead to someone they love being charged with murder."

Tommy considered Frank's words. "Then Andrew wasn't blackmailing you because of something you did?"

Frank stepped out of the stream and onto the bank. He retrieved his jacket from the bench and fished inside his pockets until he found his pipe. Lighting it, he finally turned back around to Tommy. "Jane was very ill as a young woman."

"Lots of people are ill. What was it about the illness you wanted to keep quiet?"

Frank sucked on the stem of his pipe. "Not long after we were married, Jane was to have a child. Things did not progress as expected. Afterwards, Jane spent a long time in a sanatorium."

"And the Marquess wanted you to pay for his silence?"

"Jane has never been very strong. She would have been devastated if people knew about her time away."

"Wasn't it obvious she wasn't at home?"

"I told people she was abroad." Frank sat on the bench. "We both know how the society we are a part of works. Polite people do not ask too many questions. They enquire after someone's health, are given an answer, then the conversation moves on. People may have guessed where Jane really was, but they didn't know."

"Andrew would have made sure people did?"

"I never doubted it for a moment. And, even today, I don't."

"Surely he hasn't been blackmailing you all these years?"

"Until I had no more money to give him. I sold what I could, and when he realised he wasn't getting anything more out of me, he stopped demanding money."

"But you remained friends? You visited each other's homes? I don't understand."

"Have you ever been desperate for anything in your life?" Frank demanded.

"Certainly I have." Tommy wiggled his toes in the refreshing stream. He couldn't imagine ever wanting to leave the cool paradise. "I was desperate to marry Evelyn. Then I was desperately keen to get home safely from war and be with her again."

"You would do anything for your wife?"

"I would."

"Me too," Frank said sadly. "Jane likes to ride. Of course, we have other friends who invite us, but the Marquess really does have the best hunt."

"You allowed him to bully you so Jane could ride?" It seemed a little farfetched to Tommy.

"Imagine the one thing your wife loves more than anything else," Frank encouraged. "Can you imagine it?"

Tommy swallowed. "Yes."

"Now imagine how she would feel if that was taken away from her. What would you do?"

"Whatever I could to give that back to her."

"And if that wasn't possible?"

Tommy struggled to find the right words. If he took away the children Evelyn loved so much, what would be left for her? The answer was obvious: her dogs. "I'd find the next best thing."

For Evelyn, that was her beloved Gordon Setters. For Jane, it was riding a horse.

"Do you see now?"

He did. He saw very clearly. This was a man who would do anything for the love of his wife. A man just like him. "You agreed to be his best man so Jane could carry on riding?"

"Pathetic, isn't it?" Frank tapped his pipe on the edge of the bench. "Here I am a grown man, but beholden to a man I detest."

Tommy would not embarrass Frank further by asking about his personal finances. Horses were exceedingly expensive to keep, and Frank had already intimated that he had given much of his money away years ago to keep his wife's secret.

"I'm looking into the murder of a man who, it appears, had no redeemable qualities whatsoever."

Frank put a hand over his eyes to shade them from the sun as he looked at Tommy with an intensity that made him shiver despite the heat. "It would probably be best for everyone that you let the Marquess's death lie. No good can come of it, mark my words."

"Can you tell me where you went after dinner last night?"

"After we rejoined the ladies, I went into the billiard room for a smoke." Frank shrugged.

"Did you see anyone there?"

"There was no one in the room, so far as I could tell. The

doors were open to the terrace. I stood in the cool evening air, smoked my pipe, then went back to the drawing room."

That seemed to be precisely what Constance had seen. He didn't seem to be getting anywhere with his questions.

~

"*H*ere we are, Lady Northmoor." Mrs Chapman, the housekeeper, placed a heavily laden tea tray onto a table on the terrace outside the billiard room.

"Where is everyone?" Evelyn asked.

"The staff are being interviewed, My Lady," Mrs Chapman explained. "Lady Beatrice is taking an afternoon nap, Mrs Christie is waiting for the doctor, Mrs Simmons is in the library—she didn't want to come outside. The four young ladies are in the nursery with the baby and Lady Victoria."

"Just us three then." Evelyn smiled at Frances Lester and Aunt Em.

"Any more than two or three people makes a conversation very difficult, I find," Aunt Em said with a glance at Evelyn. Her meaning was clear—Evelyn would find it difficult to question Frances if there were lots of ladies present.

"Is Mrs Christie feeling unwell?"

"I'm afraid so, My Lady, it seems she has taken the death of the Marquess of York very hard."

"I expect she has taken the fact she will not be a Marchioness harder." Aunt Em peered at Evelyn over the top of her teacup.

Mrs Chapman's lips twitched, and she turned to Evelyn. "Will that be all, My Lady?"

"Yes, thank you, Mrs Chapman. Perhaps you would let me know when the doctor arrives, please?"

"Of course." The housekeeper walked back into the house, leaving Evelyn, Aunt Em, and Frances to enjoy their tea.

Evelyn adjusted the wide-brimmed hat that was

supposed to be shading her from the sun. The sea breeze that often took away her breath with its intensity was absent and nothing moved in the garden except for butterflies and bees.

"Ah, Evelyn," Aunt Em said. "You asked me if I could find something out for you from my friends in India. I managed to verify the information you wanted clarifying."

"Goodness, that sounds rather intriguing," Frances commented.

"Would it surprise you dreadfully to know that your husband's full name is Nicholas Lester Parsons?"

Frances put a hand out to rest on the table in front of her as though she needed to hold onto to something to regain her equilibrium. "That's ridiculous."

"I thought so too, dear," Aunt Em said with one of her imperious looks. "I thought Evelyn had gone quite mad. But it seems, Lady Frances, that she was correct. Though I suppose the correct way of addressing you now is as the Marchioness of York. Shall you pour?"

Frances blinked rapidly and looked at Aunt Em and then Evelyn. "How can this be?"

"Your father's youngest brother Reginald's eldest child is your husband."

"But..."

"If you are too befuddled to pour, shall I do it?" Em offered.

"Yes, Lady Emily, thank you."

Unless Frances was the world's greatest actress, she did not know her husband's hidden identity. Though, of course, that was just supposition on Evelyn's part. Although it was true she had tried to find proof of Nicholas's parentage, there was no record of it at the India Office in London. Compulsory registration of births did not exist in India until fairly recently, so if a record existed, it was somewhere in that country. Should Nicholas intend to make a claim for the title and estate, it seemed likely he would have to take it to the chancery court to prove his entitlement.

Aunt Em passed a teacup to Frances, then passed one to Evelyn, before taking her own. "Are you feeling quite well?"

"I simply can't believe what you're telling me." Frances shook her head. "It's quite extraordinary."

"It is rather," Aunt Em agreed. "But it would mean you can stay in your home."

"You don't understand," Frances said. "Nicholas is completely penniless. We only have an income because Les gave him a job."

"Your father…" Evelyn began.

"Lady Northmoor," Frances said, her voice stronger now as she battled to regain her composure. "As Lady Emily pointed out in our previous conversation, my father was not in a financially secure position. Death duties being what they are, I simply don't see how we could keep the house."

Evelyn sipped her tea and tried to think of a way to introduce the death of the Marquess into their discussion. It wasn't a fair topic, especially given Frances's obvious shock. Could she really now insinuate that the poor woman's husband may have killed her father so he would inherit? She tried to think back to what Nicholas had said to her earlier.

She had believed he meant to keep his true identity secret, so they did not suspect him of the murder. Now, she wondered if perhaps it was because he never intended to let it be known that he was the Marquess's heir. What good would it be to have a grand title, but no estate, and no money? Maybe Nicholas was happy to go on as the manager of Les's coal mine with his modest income, but with his pride intact?

The guilt she now felt at the way she and Aunt Em had tricked Frances played on her mind. Perhaps it would have been kinder to keep Nicholas's secret. Except the police needed another suspect. If they knew about Nicholas's real identity, it was possible they would concentrate their efforts on him instead of Harry.

"Let us talk about something else," Evelyn suggested. "I am weary of death and discussing murderous plots. I'm sure you are, too…"

"Frances," she said. "Please just call me Lady Frances, as you always have. I couldn't bear for Beatrice to overhear you referring to me in any other way. She must hear the news from me."

"Of course," Evelyn murmured.

"I should find her." Frances put the teacup on the table. "Your housekeeper said she was sleeping. I will talk to Nicholas first, and then my sister."

As Frances walked back toward the house, she stopped and looked up. When she turned back to Evelyn, her face had lost all colour. She pointed, her mouth working as though she were trying valiantly to speak.

Evelyn looked up in the direction Frances had indicated. A bedroom window was flung wide open and Beatrice standing with her back to it. Suddenly, she turned around and in one swift movement, she was flying toward the terrace.

A loud shriek tore through the air, followed by a sickening thump as Beatrice hit the stone floor.

Frances stared at the body of her sister and this time when she opened her mouth, it was to let out a wail of pure distress that pierced the still summer day.

Evelyn hurried over to Frances and turned the other woman away from her sister, and led her back toward the house.

Within moments, people came running from all directions. Frank arrived, closely followed by Les and Nicholas. Jane came next, holding a book, with a look of horror on her face. Sir Richard brought up the rear.

A uniformed policeman put his whistle to his lips and blew. The shrill sound mixed with the screams from Frances increased both the urgency of the moment and the sudden mayhem caused by Beatrice's fall.

As she tried to comfort the distraught woman, Evelyn amended her perception of the situation. Beatrice hadn't fallen. She had been shoved out of the window—and with some force.

# CHAPTER 9

*T*ommy, Evelyn, and Aunt Em sat in the library with the door to the hallway closed. Huddling around the unlit fire, Evelyn blew her nose before looking at Tommy. "What now?"

Em was visibly shocked and seemed to have aged a decade since he last saw her. Evelyn was very distressed, her hands shook, and each time he thought she had stopped crying, tears fell from her eyes anew.

This was terrible, and by far the worst thing that could have happened. Everyone would look to him for guidance, and he had nothing to offer. They had spent the day trying to find out who the murderer could be and, instead of finding out who it could be, there was another body.

"At least the police won't be able to blame this on poor Harry," Aunt Em said.

"Poor Les," Evelyn said. "Oh goodness, her poor children."

A knock sounded before the door opened and the vicar, John Capes, came into the room, his cane tapping on the floor. "I'm terribly sorry to interrupt, My Lord, but is there anything I can do?"

"If you can offer some spiritual fortification, I think it would be extremely well received," Aunt Em said firmly. "Tommy is about to blame himself, and Evelyn is only a step behind him."

John closed the door and strolled over to them. "Now, how can this possibly be your fault?"

"Frances told Evelyn that Beatrice had overheard a man arguing with their father the night he was killed."

"I don't see how that is linked," John patted his forehead with a folded handkerchief. "Good grief, it's jolly hot today."

"We should have protected Beatrice," Tommy said. "If we had, she wouldn't be dead."

"Isn't that the police's job?"

"I don't know if Frances told the police what her sister overheard." Evelyn drew in a deep breath and stuffed her own hankie up her sleeve.

"And neither of them said who the person was arguing with the Marquess?"

"No," Tommy confirmed. "It's possible, of course, that the argument has nothing to do with the murder. Anything is possible. Only now Beatrice is dead, it seems the murderer has killed the person who could have identified him."

"How would the murderer have known Beatrice overheard the argument?" John asked logically.

Tommy wished fervently failing to protect Beatrice was the worst of his failings, but it wasn't. "I spoke to Constance and Grace about it. Constance was overheard talking to the Earl of Chesden in the billiard room. I asked if she had seen anyone else in the area at the time. I told her Lady Beatrice was in that room."

"I'm a little slow," the vicar said. "I still don't think I completely understand."

"The killer must have overheard the conversation I had with my sisters. I spoke with them in the billiard room, but the doors to the terrace were open. Once he knew he could be identified as the person who argued with the Marquess shortly before his death, he immediately becomes the most likely suspect."

"People really are rather silly," Aunt Em observed. "Why didn't whoever it was just come forward, admit to a blazing row with the Marquess, and that would have been that. An argument isn't proof of a more serious crime."

"You're right," Evelyn agreed. "Now it's obvious whoever was involved in the argument killed the Marquess, otherwise there would be no need for Beatrice to die."

"He panicked," Tommy said.

"Or she."

Tommy looked at Evelyn and raised an eyebrow. "She?"

She met his gaze. "Why not?"

"Stabbing and pushing a person out of a window are not crimes usually associated with a female killer."

"Have you forgotten Edith Billingham?"

"Are there any female suspects left?"

Evelyn and Aunt Em looked at him expectantly. Tommy eventually realised what they were both too polite to put into words. "There's my mother."

"Oh surely not," John said. "Mrs Christie couldn't possibly have killed her own fiancé."

"I'm afraid you're entirely too kind and forgiving," Aunt Em said. "Though I don't think it's Helen. She was so looking forward to becoming the Marchioness of York I can't believe she'd literally kill her chance of gaining that title."

"Who does that leave us with?" Evelyn asked.

"Les and Nicholas, Frank and Jane Simmons."

"Your mother and Sir Richard," Aunt Em added. "Think logically, my boy, you're always telling me there's an unknown factor and you can't rule anyone out until you know what that is. No matter their relationship to you, or how much you like them."

"It's hard," Tommy admitted. "If only I'd spoken to the

girls in here. With the doors shut. Or simply mentioned Constance had been overheard, but not said by whom."

"You are not to blame for the actions of someone else," the vicar said firmly. "Remember, we all have a set of guidelines we should live by but, equally, we all are given free agency to make our own decisions. You did not choose to kill the Marquess, or Lady Beatrice. The killer did. You bear no responsibility for his or her actions."

"I hear your argument, John, but if I'd made better choices Beatrice would not be lying dead outside on our terrace. I don't know how Frances will ever recover from witnessing her sister's death."

"I should expect two bodies in one day is rather a lot for your wife to cope with," Aunt Em said caustically.

"Perhaps we should stop." Tommy looked at Evelyn's pale face. "I imagine Detective Inspector Andrews will come straight back here as soon as he hears the news. We should leave it up to the police to find the killer."

Aunt Em clapped her hands. "I agree. I do so hate the two of you putting yourself in harm's way. It's bad enough there is a killer on the loose in the house, but do you two have to go poking that lunatic with a stick until he attacks one of you next?"

"The police haven't done so well in the past, have they?" Evelyn retorted. "For instance, we know who the next Marquess of York will be. The police don't even know that person is in the house. They haven't even examined that angle."

"You think we should go on?"

"Don't you?"

"Thomas Christie, I demand you put your own, and Evelyn's, safety first and stop this nonsense. I forbid you to continue."

Evelyn leaned over and kissed Aunt Em's cheek, then took the old lady's hands in her own. "We must do this.

Hopefully, the police will see that the two murders were committed by the same person and free Harry because, of course, he couldn't have committed the second. But we can't be sure that will happen. Let us bring this to an end, Tommy."

"I need to put right what I have done wrong."

"Then we shall have a surprise for you, Aunt Em." Evelyn squeezed Em's hands with her own. "So please let us solve these murders with your blessing. Then I promise we shall have the biggest and best party this old house has ever seen."

"Am I invited?"

Tommy grinned. "You are an absolute necessity for the success of the party, John."

"Then let us pray for your safety, and for God to arm you both with the wisdom and perseverance you shall need to bring this unseemly incident to a satisfactory conclusion."

~

"*M*rs Christie, may I come in?" Evelyn chewed her lip nervously. Helen may have been her mother-in-law for over six years, but she had never been invited to call her by her forename.

"What is going on outside?"

"If I can come in, I could tell you?"

The door was pulled open, and Helen stood back to allow Evelyn to enter her bedroom. The bed was mussed, the fire in the hearth blazing, and one curtain was slightly open. Helen looked through the crack in the curtains. "Why are the police stomping all over your lawn?"

"I'm sorry to tell you that there has been another murder."

Helen clutched the edges of her wrap against her throat with shaking fingers. "Who is dead?"

"Lady Beatrice."

"What happened to her?" Helen sat on a chair next to the

window but made no move to open the curtains or a window, even though the heat was stifling.

"It appears that she was pushed out of a bedroom window."

"Pu…pushed? Could she have stumbled?"

Evelyn pointed at the window beside Helen. "It's only really possible to fall out if one were to sit on the ledge, lean backwards, and lose their balance."

"She may have been doing exactly that," Helen said stubbornly.

"I was outside when the incident happened. One moment she was standing next to the window with her back to it, then she turned around abruptly and was propelled out of the opening with some force."

Helen shivered despite the overwhelming heat. "How dreadful."

Despite the woman's behaviour earlier in the day, Evelyn felt sorry for Helen. "Yes, it is. This must be a terrible shock for you on top of Andrew's death."

Helen's eyes widened, and she reached forward and grasped Evelyn's arm. "Do you think someone is killing the entire family one by one?"

"I can't think of a single reason why anyone would do that." Helen's hands were icy cold on Evelyn's skin. "Please try not to worry. The police will certainly step up their protection of everyone in the house until the killer is caught."

Helen's lower lip trembled. "I'm up here all alone."

"I know it must be very difficult for you, but perhaps it would be best if you dressed and came downstairs? It will be easier for the police to keep us safe if we are together rather than in separate rooms."

"I don't think I can do that." Helen released her grip on Evelyn and lifted a handful of hair. "Look at me. I am an absolute wreck."

"I'm sure your maid can soon have you looking your

usual glamorous self. Shall I send Doris to your room? She is a whizz at dressing hair."

Helen scrutinised Evelyn's hair before answering. "No thank you, dear."

Evelyn wasn't sure if she was glad 'old Helen' was back. It was a relief to hear her mother-in-law talking in her usual disagreeable way, but what had caused her to be so afraid? Evelyn was certain it was fear making Helen's hands shake, and feel as though she'd made snowballs without wearing mittens.

"Have you been upstairs in your room since you received the news about Andrew?"

"I'm hardly likely to go anywhere looking like this, am I?" Helen retorted sarcastically.

"If you don't want to come downstairs with everyone else, maybe I can send someone to sit up here with you?"

Helen sat back in her chair and folded her hands in her lap. "I'm not a child and I don't need a nursemaid."

"I don't want you alone and frightened."

"Why do you care?" Helen challenged.

It would have been easy to answer that she would take the same care over anyone who stayed in her house because that was the truth, but Evelyn tried to work on Helen's maternal instinct. It might be buried deeply, but surely it was there somewhere?

"Tommy loves you very much. He would much rather you were downstairs and safe than up here by yourself."

"This modern way of talking about one's feelings isn't something we do in our family."

"I'm sure Constance and Grace would benefit from your presence."

One of Helen's hands flew to her chest. "What about my poor Harry?"

"There hasn't been time to speak to Detective Inspector Andrews's colleague, but Tommy is hopeful Harry will be immediately released as it isn't possible he committed the second murder."

"But then he will be in danger."

Evelyn couldn't understand Helen's thought process. She didn't seem at all interested in her daughters, yet seemed horrified at the idea of Harry returning to Hessleham Hall. "Why would Harry be in danger?"

"The murderer is killing people close to me, don't you see that?" Helen shrieked.

"I didn't know you were particularly friendly with Beatrice." Evelyn couldn't help the slightly sardonic note that crept into her voice.

"You wouldn't understand," Helen said scathingly.

"That beautiful set of handkerchiefs that the Marquess gave you," Evelyn said, changing the subject. It wasn't worth arguing with Helen. She didn't think the other woman would ever see anyone else's point above her own. "Do you have any missing?"

"You cannot think someone would take one of my handkerchiefs? What sort of household do you run? If one of your staff has been seen with one, I insist they are dismissed immediately."

Evelyn held in a deep sigh. Helen was incredibly infuriating and difficult to deal with. She couldn't tell Helen the truth, but she wanted an answer to her question. "Would you mind checking for me, please?"

With a great show of impatience, Helen flounced over to the chest of drawers and yanked open the top one. "There should be six. I count only four."

"I gave you one earlier today. Have you used another one since your arrival?"

Helen blinked, then smiled brightly at Evelyn. "Yes, I put one in my bag last night before dinner."

Her mother-in-law wasn't a very good liar. Whether that

was because she knew exactly what had happened to the missing hankie, or because she was protecting whoever had it, Evelyn didn't know. She thought back to the first murder that happened at Hessleham Hall the previous year. Sometimes guilt affected people in different ways. Perhaps what Evelyn perceived as Helen being afraid was a sign of the immense guilt the other woman felt after committing two murders.

A knock on the door interrupted Evelyn's thoughts, and she walked over to the door to open it.

"Lady Northmoor!" Doctor Theodore Mainwaring greeted Evelyn. "What a pleasant surprise. I understand Mrs Christie called for me?"

Evelyn stepped through the door. "Do you remember what happened to Isobel Turnbull last year?"

"Why, of course."

"Please don't leave Helen with sleeping draughts."

Teddy frowned and nodded. "You're worried about what she may do with them?"

"I'm very concerned about Helen. She seems very afraid. Would it be terribly unethical if I asked you not to give her something to make her sleepy?"

Teddy smiled wryly. "I think you know the answer to that."

"If she requests something to calm her nerves or make her sleep, is there something you can give her that will only last a few hours? I can send someone up to sit with her to ensure her safety."

"You truly are seriously troubled about her safety, aren't you?"

"I'm not sure at this stage of our investigations whether my fear is for Helen's safety or that of others."

"Does Tommy think his mother is a suspect?" Teddy whispered, not only because he referred to his friend informally, but so he was not overheard.

"He accepts we cannot rule her out." Evelyn lifted a shoulder. "But I don't think he believes she is capable of such evil."

"I shouldn't think anyone would want to accept murder was an act their mother could carry out."

"How is Isolde?" Evelyn changed the subject, and she really wanted to know how her friend was.

"Her ankles are swollen, she has to get up several times in the night to use the facilities, she can't get comfortable, and in this heat, she says she feels like a steamed pudding." Teddy grimaced. "But she also says she's never been happier."

"Send her my love and very best wishes," Evelyn said. "And—"

"Yes," Teddy interrupted. "I know. The minute I have any news, I am to telephone you immediately."

Evelyn smiled. "Thank you. I couldn't be more excited for you both."

~

"Can't this wait?" Nicholas Lester snapped at Tommy. "My wife is distraught. She has lost both her father and her sister in one day. The latter right in front of her eyes."

"I'm afraid if we don't catch the murderer soon, he could strike again."

"He?"

"Figure of speech," Tommy clarified. "Can we talk? I shall be quick so you can get back to your wife."

"Your village doctor sedated her." Nicholas slumped into a chair in the library, all fight gone out of him. "But I should still like to sit with her."

"My wife tells me you stand to inherit. Is that right?"

Nicholas rested his chin on his upturned palm. "I was trying to keep it quiet, so I wasn't suspected of killing Andrew." Nicholas gave an ironic laugh. "Of course, I wasn't allowed to call him that. He insisted I call him 'My Lord'. Do you think he would've treated me any better if he knew I was his heir presumptive?"

"No, I shouldn't have thought so," Tommy answered honestly. "Why didn't you tell anyone?"

"Father didn't have positive memories of growing up on the family estate. After he served in the Boer War, he didn't return to England. He travelled to India and worked as a Christian missionary. Father regretted his time in the Army and was a powerful advocate for peace for the rest of his life." Nicholas lifted his head. "In contrast, I had a wonderful childhood in India, but I couldn't help wondering if I was missing out on knowing my family."

"You returned to England for that reason?"

"Yes." Nicholas nodded. "I wanted to know my father's family. Although Andrew was a thoroughly unpleasant individual, I met and fell in love with Frances."

"She doesn't know?"

"Frances has absolutely no idea." Nicholas looked up. "I will have to tell her."

"Only if you choose to accept your birthright."

"Is there a reason I shouldn't?"

Tommy had no hesitation. "I have never rued my own inheritance. Even though I work long hours, I see it as my duty to run the estate to the best of my ability and leave it as prosperous as I can for the next generation. But if you were going to do the same, why have you kept your identity secret?"

"I spoke to Clara, Frances's mother, before I proposed. She begged me not to tell Frances, but especially not Andrew."

Tommy frowned. "Why? What difference did she think it would make?"

"She was frightened that Andrew would use the knowledge to drive a wedge between Beatrice and Frances. They have always been exceptionally close, you see. Beatrice is the eldest, but it would be Frances that would eventually run the house because of being married to me."

"That sounds like the type of thing that Andrew would do."

"Clara favoured me telling no one and letting the title fall into extinction."

"Did she blame the title for Andrew's behaviour?"

"I think she did. Despite his cruelty, I think she still believed there was some good in him, but the power the title gave him squashed it."

"Do you believe that?"

"Absolutely not," Nicholas said stridently. "There wasn't a bit of good in that man. The way he treated his wife and children bordered on criminal."

"Did you argue with Andrew last night?"

"No, I didn't. I endeavoured to keep a peace between us," Nicholas explained. "In case one day I wished to make myself known."

"I apologise for asking this next question, but I must ask it of everyone." Tommy shuffled his feel awkwardly. "Where were you when Beatrice died?"

"In the garden," Nicholas said quickly. "I heard Frances scream. I suppose everyone did, the poor darling. I came running to see what had happened immediately."

Nicholas had placed himself outside of the house, but was he telling the truth? Tommy had no reason to doubt the other man's word, but neither did he have any evidence to prove he hadn't killed Beatrice. The only people who could be in the clear for that murder were Evelyn, Aunt Em, and Frances. Anyone else could have slipped into the bedroom, argued with Beatrice, and then pushed her out.

A thought occurred to Tommy, and he was furious with himself that he hadn't considered it before. Had Beatrice been in her own bedroom when she was pushed, or in someone else's? Did that matter to the investigation—he supposed it did if she was pushed from the window of the murderer's room.

He must go out onto the lawn, work out which bedroom window was wide open, then determine whose room that was.

"Thank you for your time," Tommy said. "Please pass on my and Lady Northmoor's sincere condolences to your wife."

# CHAPTER 10

"Mr Dawson, is there anything we can do for you? Anything at all that you need?" Evelyn approached Beatrice's widower, who sat on one of the chairs in the billiard room. He looked out across the terrace to the scene of his wife's death.

He looked at her for a moment as though he had no comprehension of who she was. "Oh, Lady Northmoor, hullo."

"May I sit with you?"

He shrugged and looked back out through the open doors. One uniformed police officer stood next to Beatrice's body, which had been covered by a white sheet. "She didn't deserve to die."

"No, of course she didn't," Evelyn said soothingly. "You should know that she may have had information that could have uncovered the Marquess's killer."

"Beatrice?" The look of surprise on Les's face could not have been manufactured.

"She told Frances that she overheard an argument between her father and someone else on the night of his death. Unfortunately, she did not reveal the name of that person."

"You think she was killed to keep her quiet?"

"It would seem so."

"She didn't tell Frances who their father was arguing with?"

"I rather hoped she had told you."

Les shook his head. "I'm sorry to disappoint you, Lady Northmoor, but she didn't even tell me she had heard her father arguing. Though if she had, I probably wouldn't have taken much notice. There was barely a day went by when the Marquess didn't disagree with someone."

"I'm desperately sorry to ask," Evelyn said hesitantly. "But would you mind awfully telling me where you have been this afternoon?"

He blinked, then lifted a shoulder in total resignation. "I have nothing to hide. I spoke to your husband in the stables, then came back to the house. Beatrice and I had lunch together, then she said she needed to lie down. She didn't really like her father, you know that, but his death was still a terrible shock. After that, I spoke to Frank Simmons in the billiard room then went for a walk in the garden."

"Is that where you were when your wife—"

"Was killed?" Les asked bitterly. "Yes, I was walking in your beautiful garden while some fiend was upstairs throwing my wife out of our bedroom window."

"Oh, that can't be right." Evelyn frowned. "I can't believe I didn't think of this earlier."

"What isn't right?"

"It wasn't your bedroom window."

Les looked up as though trying to visualise the corridor above in relation to where Beatrice had landed on the terrace and the position of their room. "Our bedroom did not overlook the terrace."

"No, your room is a little farther along," Evelyn confirmed.

"Who is staying in that room?"

"I really don't know," Evelyn lied. "I will check with our housekeeper. She will know."

"When you have that information, then you shall know the culprit."

"Not necessarily," Evelyn said. "All we will know is who should've been in that room. We don't know why Beatrice was in there, or who she was with in there."

"Are you suggesting she was having an assignation with another chap?"

"Oh, my dear Mr Dawson, absolutely not. I am more afraid that someone lured her into the room to find out what she knew."

"Beatrice was rather trusting." Les covered his face with his hands. "The Marquess was constantly telling her she was stupid. She wasn't. But she did have a tendency to see the good in people who didn't deserve it."

"It sounds to me that your wife had a very sweet nature," Evelyn said. "Is there anything else you can tell me? Anything that may be relevant. Or, even something that seems inconsequential, but different in Beatrice's behaviour the last couple of days?"

"She was on edge," Les told her, dropping his hands and wrinkling his forehead. "Beatrice didn't want to come for the wedding. It wasn't just that she didn't like your mother-in-law. She wouldn't have liked anyone that she saw as taking her mother's place."

"On edge? How so?"

"Nervous." Les closed his eyes. "It sounds silly, but it was as though she couldn't sit still. Almost like she was waiting for something to happen."

"Could Beatrice have killed her father?"

"Yes," Les replied without hesitation. "But, as I said to

Lord Northmoor earlier, so could any of us. There wasn't a single person here in the house who liked him. Other than the guests on your side of the family who didn't know him."

"Did you know Sir Richard before this weekend?"

"No, never met him." Les pulled a handkerchief out of his pocket and patted his eyes. "I've heard of him, of course, but I've never spent much time in London and I understand he spends most of his time there and rarely comes to the country."

"Yes, that seems to be so." Evelyn got to her feet. She felt terrible questioning Les while he was so raw, but it had to be done. "I shall leave you, but please, do let me know if there's anything we can do for you."

"I should just like the police to allow me to take my wife home." Les covered his face again and sobbed loudly into his handkerchief.

Evelyn sat back down and whispered what she hoped were comforting words while her mind raced with the new information she had learned—Beatrice had been in the bedroom assigned to Frank and Jane Simmons and, according to her husband, had seemed nervous before her father had even been killed.

She hated how little sense everything made. Why would Beatrice follow the person she knew had argued with her father into a room that didn't belong to her? Surely she would've known how dangerous it was to be alone with that person?

~

"*L*ord Northmoor," Alexander Ryder said, somewhat stiffly. "Would it be convenient for me to speak to you?"

"Would you care to join me in a drink?" Tommy asked,

moving over to the drink cabinet. It had been an interminably long day, although it was only midafternoon.

"Yes, thank you. Just a small brandy for me."

Alex stood in the middle of the room, his hands behind his back, as he rocked gently backward and forward. Tommy poured them both a drink, then retook his seat. "Sit down, man, you're making me nervous."

"It's me who is nervous."

"I find that hard to believe." Tommy wished he could take the words back as soon as he'd said them. Although they were the truth, they were impolite, and that wasn't like him at all.

"I expect I deserved that. I made rather a fool of myself in London."

"You were a little insufferable."

"I've changed," he said earnestly. "Father was a difficult man. I'm afraid I allowed his character to form my own. I'm not that person anymore."

"Did you come to that conclusion before or after the social invitations dried up?" Tommy raised a quizzical eyebrow.

Alex gave a dry chuckle. "Again, I suppose I deserve that. As you are aware, London has not been a particularly kind place since my father's trial."

Despite his low opinion of Alex, Tommy couldn't help but have some sympathy for the man. Although he hadn't endeared himself to anyone during his stay at their house in Belgrave Square, Alex had experienced great tribulations because of his father's actions. He himself had committed no crime, but because his father had, polite society wanted nothing to do with the Ryder family.

"I'm sure it is only a matter of time before there is some other scandal and the mothers of young ladies in London will suddenly remember that you are the Earl of Chesden and, not only that, but you have a particularly beautiful estate in the west of England and a splendid property in Ireland."

"I'd rather they didn't remember those things."

"Really?" Tommy considered Alex. "Why is that?"

Alex ran a finger along the back of his collar. "It's excessively warm in here."

Tommy suppressed a grin. It wouldn't be kind to show his amusement at the other man's discomfort, but it was tempting. "It's a hot summer day."

"Indeed." Alex picked up his drink and drank a generous portion. He cleared his throat, then coughed. His face turned red, and he tried to cough again.

"I say," Tommy said. "Are you alright?"

"Went down the wrong way," Alex gasped. He wiped his eyes, which had started to water. "Gosh, I feel like such a fool. I came to talk to you, man to man, and now I'm crying like a child."

Tommy smiled now, feeling more at ease with Alex. "Just calm down and say what you would like to say. I promise I'm not nearly as much of an ogre as you seem to think I am."

"It's not that," Alex said earnestly, and took a sip of his drink. "It is simply that I would like to ask you something and I am very much afraid you will turn me down flat before really considering my question."

"I like to think that I'm a fair man," Tommy said.

"I would like to court your sister," Alex said, speaking so quickly that his words ran together. "That is, your sister Constance. She's clever, and funny, not to mention incredibly beautiful. I would like your permission to court her."

"Constance is very much her own person," Tommy said carefully. "I spoke to her earlier as I was told you were alone in the billiard room with her last night."

Alex held his hands in front of his body. "We were just talking. I would never—"

"I don't think 'never' is true."

Alex flushed slightly. "I told you, Northmoor," he said defensively. "I am a different man now. I respect your sister."

"I should hope you do." Tommy looked at Alex mildly. "Because if you didn't, you can be sure I would chase you off my land with a loaded shotgun."

"Yes sir." Alex picked up his glass. "May I have your permission?"

"You should know that Constance will not be living with our mother anymore. She is to move into Hessleham Hall with myself and Evelyn. We intend to strictly chaperone my sisters. There will be no sneaking off to other rooms of the house. What happened in Belgrave Square will not be happening at Hessleham Hall. I demand your deference to my high moral standards."

Tommy nearly cringed as he finished his mini speech. He sounded like an old man. No, he sounded like a concerned father. Was this what it would be like to have that level of responsibility for another person?

"Yes, Lord Northmoor," Alex answered in a voice with no trace of his usual arrogance. Perhaps he was telling the truth, and he had indeed changed.

"I am prepared to give you the benefit of the doubt." Tommy pointed at him. "But, one wrong step and—"

"Yes, I remember." Alex grinned. "You will chase me from Hessleham with a gun in your hands."

"I'm a rather good shot," Tommy told him. "Why don't you stay on here after this weekend? Shooting season starts soon and perhaps I can prove to you the accuracy of my shooting?"

"Thank you for the invitation. I accept."

Tommy softened his tone. "It will also give you some time to get to know my sister a little better. Once you know how headstrong and opinionated Constance is, you may change your mind about courting her."

"Thank you." Alex put out his hand and Tommy shook it, feeling exactly how he imagined any caretaker of a young woman felt—nervous, hopeful, and incredibly protective.

"Now, about that other matter? Have you been able to arrange it?"

"Yes." Alex grinned. "David told me what was needed, and I telephoned to my friend. I have received word back that the arrangements have been made. I have instructed my bank to furnish my friend with the required cheque."

"Splendid." Tommy sat back in his chair. Evelyn would be very pleased. "Now all we must do is wrap up this ghastly business and your brother can marry the girl he loves."

"He deserves it," Alex said warmly. "My brother has always been a much better fellow than me. If only Hugh could be here. He will be desperately sad to miss the occasion."

"I've had some ideas about Hugh's situation," Tommy said. "Once this business is concluded, I should like to speak to you and David about my thoughts."

A movement outside the window caught Tommy's eye, and he twisted so he could see more clearly. "Is that my sister out there?"

"Yes, My Lord," Alex answered with a smile that took over his entire face. "I'm afraid it is. I told Constance I was coming to speak to you and asked her to wait for me in the drawing room with her sister and Lady Emily."

"As you can see," Tommy waved a hand in the direction of the window, "my sister has done exactly what she wants and completely disregarded your words."

"Yes, I know." Alex's smile broadened. "Isn't it marvellous?"

That wasn't quite the word that Tommy would've used, but he did understand Alex's point. He had likely become bored with girls who did exactly what he said when he asked them to. Constance was much more likely to do the complete opposite, just because she could.

The world was changing and, for women like his sister, Tommy was very glad it was.

~

*E*velyn sat next to Tommy and across the desk from Detective Inspector Andrews and Detective Sergeant Montgomery.

"Have you worked it out yet?" Andrews asked without preamble.

"Not yet," she snapped. "Though it certainly isn't for lack of trying."

"Are you suggesting we haven't tried, Lady Northmoor?"

"You arrested an innocent young boy and took him to York to be questioned who'd done nothing wrong other than drink too much."

Her words were uncharacteristically curt, but what did he expect? Not only had she been the one to find Andrew's body, but Beatrice had died in front of her eyes. She didn't think she would ever get that sight out of her mind.

"That young boy was heard threatening the victim."

"Are you still refusing to tell us who told you that?" Tommy demanded.

"Yes," he confirmed. "It's a police investigation. I don't need to share any of the information we have learned with you."

"I am sure we know more than you." Evelyn immediately regretted her words, which sounded petulant and childish.

The detective leaned forward on the desk. "I agreed with your husband at the commencement of this case that you would share with me anything that you learned."

"And we shall honour that agreement." Tommy rubbed Evelyn's knee. "Won't we, darling?"

"Fine," she snapped. "Nicholas Lester is the heir presumptive to the Marquess of York."

The detective frowned. "Nicholas Lester? But shouldn't his surname be Parsons for that to work?"

"He uses his mother's surname," Evelyn said flatly. "But

you will struggle to find proof of his identity as birth records in India are not compulsory."

"I've spoken with him," Tommy went on. "He isn't sure if he will even claim the title."

"You don't think he killed the Marquess?"

"I don't think he killed him to inherit," Tommy said. "I didn't say he isn't who we are looking for."

Detective Inspector Andrews frowned. "What other motive could he have?"

"You must be aware from the interviews you have carried out that the Marquess was a thoroughly unpleasant man. Any number of people could have killed him because they could no longer listen to his cruel comments."

"Or because his unkindness was affecting someone they love," Tommy added. "Never forget what someone will do for love. It's a very powerful motive."

"Have you ruled anyone out?" The detective looked at Evelyn. "Other than your brother-in-law, of course."

"No," she said firmly. "The only thing that has changed since you left is that Beatrice is now dead. I have heard nothing that would cause me to rule anyone out of our investigations. Have you, Tommy?"

"Our investigation." Detective Inspector Andrews pointed at himself and then Detective Sergeant Montgomery. "Us—the police detectives."

"In my mind, we still have a full cast of suspects," Tommy confirmed.

"Including your mother?"

"Yes, Detective Inspector, including my mother."

"I've looked at the body," he said then, changing the course of their conversation. "It seems very clear Lady Beatrice was pushed from an upstairs window and died immediately."

"She wasn't in her own bedroom," Evelyn supplied.

"I wondered about that when I spoke to Nicholas."

Andrews looked at Montgomery. "Get one of the staff in here. We need to find out which room Lady Beatrice was in before she died."

"There is no need for that," Evelyn said calmly. "She was in the room allocated to Frank and Jane Simmons."

"How can you be so certain?"

Evelyn eyed the detective coolly. There weren't many things she disliked more than her word being doubted or being underestimated. "It is my house and therefore my duty to know where my guests are staying. A large event such as this wedding is thoroughly organised with my staff weeks in advance."

"Do we know where they were when the murder took place?" He asked his colleague sharply.

The man floundered, and Evelyn continued. "Jane Simmons was in the library when tea was brought out to the terrace. Where she was when the murder took place, I could not say. In addition, I must tell you that although she has spent a lot of time in that room with a book in her hands, I have yet to see her read a page."

"We haven't spoken to Frank since Lady Beatrice was killed. However, I have spoken to Nicholas and Evelyn spoke to Les. They both claim to have been in the garden."

"They could be in on it together," Montgomery suggested.

Three sets of eyes looked at the junior detective. "You think Dawson killed his own wife?"

"Stranger things have happened." Montgomery stared mutinously back at his superior.

"What motive would he have?"

"To cover up the original murder," Montgomery shot back.

"Which happened because?"

"Dawson and Lester agreed to share the money when Lester becomes Marquess."

"That might work," Tommy said. "If there was money. But

there isn't. In fact, we've found that the Marquess's biggest source of income seems to have been from blackmail."

Montgomery threw his hands up in defeat. "Then it could be anyone."

"That is what we have been telling you," Evelyn said. "It's impossible to rule anyone out. One would like to think Mr Dawson didn't kill his wife, but Montgomery is right that it's possible. Without knowing what people are hiding, it's impossible to rule them in or out."

"Were the two gentlemen both in the garden?" Andrews asked.

"I will check with Malton. He usually has an excellent idea of where our guests are. But my guess is no, I don't think either of them were in the garden."

"Why not?"

"The garden is the farthest place from the house and I think they both chose that place so they wouldn't look guilty, not necessarily because they have anything to hide."

"I say, Andrews," Tommy said suddenly. "You brought my brother back with you, didn't you?"

"He went straight to the kitchen for something to eat," the detective confirmed. "Speaking of which, I'm famished. All I seem to have done today is interview and travel to York and back."

"That was rather your choice," Evelyn said tartly.

"We shall arrange for a meal to be sent for both of you," Tommy said soothingly, grabbing Evelyn's hand and giving it a squeeze. "Now, if you'll excuse us, we must see if there's anything we can do for our guests."

Evelyn followed Tommy out of his office and into the hallway. "We didn't tell them about your mother's handkerchief."

"No, we didn't." Tommy's mouth lifted in a crooked smile. "I must have forgotten to share that piece of information."

# CHAPTER 11

*T*ommy took some time to ensure Harry was alright and none too worse for his ordeal before seeking Sir Richard. The big man stood in the billiard room, looking out as the police removed Beatrice's body.

"Terrible business," he muttered.

"Quite dreadful," Tommy agreed. "I say, do you know the Earl of Chesden, or his younger brother, David? He said he recognised you, but couldn't remember where from."

"I'm a member of several gentlemen's clubs in London. Perhaps we attend the same one?" Sir Richard pulled on his moustache, as though it helped him think more clearly. "I recognise the Earl by sight, but I don't think I've been introduced to either him or his brother. On the other hand, I knew the old Earl fairly well."

Tommy shrugged, as though it was of no importance. "I'm awfully sorry, but I must ask you where you were when Beatrice died?"

"Right here." Sir Richard swept out a hand encompassing the room. "I was in one of the chairs facing the fireplace."

"I don't believe anyone saw you in here."

"No reason they would." Sir Richard pointed at the group

of chairs crowded around the unlit fireplace. He gave a self deprecating cough of laughter. "Surprised they didn't hear me snoring though."

"You were asleep?"

He laughed again. This time, it was a more natural sound. "I was. Often do after lunch, it's my age, you know. Woke with rather a jolt when that poor woman began screaming."

"That would have been Lady Frances," Tommy said. "Evelyn said Lady Beatrice died right before her poor sister's eyes."

Sir Richard tutted. "Unspeakably tragic."

"The police have brought Harry back, thank goodness."

"Oh, that is excellent news," Sir Richard brightened. "I should like to speak to the boy. It's no good drinking to excess and then not being around to protect his mother."

Tommy swallowed back the words he wanted to say: His mother hadn't been at risk of harm, so far as they knew, and she herself was willing to leave all of her children homeless to marry the Marquess! Sir Richard had known Helen since he was a teenager himself and was very fond of her, despite her very obvious character flaws.

"I've spoken to him briefly." Tommy eyed the man he'd known all his life, but somehow was only just seeing properly for the first time as an adult man—did he have some sort of romantic interest in Helen? "He's rather embarrassed, as I am sure you can imagine. He will stay on at Hessleham Hall with my sisters."

Sir Richard shook his head. "That's not right, your mother will be devastated."

"She was more than happy to leave them here when she planned to move to live with the Marquess."

"But that's not happening now," Sir Richard said. "You can't take her children away from her, you must see that would be cruel after what has happened."

Politeness stopped Tommy from telling Sir Richard that it

was none of his business. Although he was an old family friend, he wasn't family. If, perhaps, Sir Richard had been a friend of his family, Tommy might have been more inclined to listen. But as it was, he wasn't. He wanted to provide a secure home for his siblings that would not change the next time his mother decided they did not fit in with her plans.

"I find it unforgivable that she was willing to leave them behind to marry a man who had proven himself to be a thoroughly nasty individual."

Sir Richard seemed to relax, and a broad smile creased his face. "I'm sure this is a conversation you must have with your mother. My apologies for inserting myself into the family business. Your demeanour tells me quite clearly that my input is not required."

"Thank you for understanding." Tommy took a step backwards. "I do hope I haven't offended you."

"Of course not, my boy," Sir Richard said warmly. "I can't pretend to understand how families such as yours work. It's been years since I had a family of my own."

The gentle rebuke reminded Tommy that he and his siblings were the closest thing to children Sir Richard had. Still, he wasn't their father, and it wasn't up to him to decide what was best for Constance, Grace, and Harry.

❧

Frank Simmons was again sitting on the bench near the stream as Evelyn approached him. "May I join you?"

"Certainly," he replied, getting to his feet as she approached. "What brings you out here, Lady Northmoor? Sleuthing?"

"Yes," she answered. "Would you mind answering a few questions?"

Frank stuck the stem of his pipe between his teeth. "Depends on what they are."

"Your wife cannot read, can she?"

He gazed at Evelyn calmly for so long, she thought he would ignore her question. "What makes you say that?"

"I've talked to her several times in the library, and each time she has had a book on her knee. Popular books. But never once has she been reading it. The books have been closed in her lap."

"She likes the feel of them," Frank explained. "And the smell."

"I can understand that," Evelyn said. "I love those things too."

"Would you mind if I smoked?"

"Of course not. Go ahead."

Frank struck a match and lit his pipe. He puffed away on it for a few moments before addressing Evelyn again. "You won't let her secret out?"

"I can't see any reason I would ever need to discuss it with anyone else." Evelyn smiled. "But why does she spend so much time in a room she can't fully enjoy?"

Frank sighed. "I explained to your husband that Jane has had several medical issues over the years. I don't know if her difficulty in reading is because of a defect in her vision or something else. She says the words jump around the page and she can't concentrate on them fully."

"That's very sad," Evelyn said. "I love to read and can't imagine how awful it would be to pick up a book and not be able to enjoy it."

"To answer your other question, she spends a lot of her time in libraries because she thinks she should."

"I don't understand." Evelyn shook her head slightly.

"Jane thinks that women of a certain class should spend their time reading, or some other worthy pursuit. The Marquess was a bully, as you are aware, but Jane was very keen not to feel the sting of his vicious words, so she did everything she could to fit in."

"Lady Emily has trouble reading these days," Evelyn said. "Perhaps Jane would like to join us later this afternoon. I often read a little to Lady Emily before we get ready for dinner."

"That would be very kind. I'm sure Jane would be very grateful to sit with you both."

"Mr Simmons," Evelyn said briskly. "Can you tell me where you were when Lady Beatrice was killed?"

"In my room," he answered immediately, as though he had been waiting to say those words since the moment she sat down next to him. "I had run out of tobacco and so went to fetch a new pouch."

Of course, he was lying. He couldn't have been in his room, otherwise he would have seen Beatrice arguing with whoever it was that pushed her out of the window. Unless he was that person—but then why would he put himself in the very place where she was killed?

"Thank you." Evelyn got to her feet. "I'll let Jane know about the reading later."

"I would be ever so grateful, Lady Northmoor. It will thrill Jane to be included."

～

"Northmoor, how goes the plans?" David asked.

"Full speed ahead," Tommy confirmed. "We shall have this investigation tied up, our guests will leave, then you can marry Madeleine on Monday."

David breathed out a sigh of relief. "I'm so glad. I thought after all this nasty business, we wouldn't be able to marry after all."

"John asked if you're happy to marry in the chapel, or

whether you'd prefer to have the ceremony in the village church?"

"I'd marry Madeleine at the top of the Eiffel Tower." He grinned a little awkwardly. "But, given the circumstances, I think I should clarify things with her before I give you an answer."

"That's a very wise decision!" Tommy patted David on the back. "A sensible husband always discusses his ideas with his wife before they become a firm plan."

"Does this mean you've identified the murderer?"

"We're still working on it." Tommy grimaced. "It seems there's no one the Marquess didn't insult or wasn't blackmailing."

David snapped his fingers. "That's it!"

"What's it?"

"I told you I remembered that old duffer? There was some sort of scandal."

"With Sir Richard?" Tommy frowned. "That can't be right. The man is above reproach."

David held up his hands. "I'm only telling you what I know."

"More like what you think you remember."

"I'm certain of it." David closed his eyes and his brow furrowed. "It's no good, I can't remember exactly what it was."

"If it was a scandal, the whole of London would know."

"Not always. If you have money, it's possible to hush anything up. You know that."

"But London is such a hotbed of gossip."

"It's also rife with so called gentleman's agreements where people are paid under the table to forget they saw something, or to use their power and influence to cover up something that would destroy their character."

Tommy persisted. "But you can't think Sir Richard has something to hide."

CATHERINE COLES

"You're being too kind again," David said. "Everyone has something they'd rather other people not find out about themselves."

"I don't."

"Actually, Northmoor, you do." David sat in one of the chairs facing the door of the billiard room. "Sit down and I shall reveal all."

Tommy walked around the room before settling in the chair next to David's. "It appears this is a room where people sit in chairs and listen to other people's conversations."

"Really? How sneaky. Where are people's manners these days? Shouldn't one make themselves known if someone else enters a room?"

"I suppose if they are up to no good, they keep quiet." Tommy drew a cigar out of the inner pocket of his jacket. "Will you have one?"

"Actually," David said. "I think I shall."

Tommy picked up the matches from the table and lit his cigar, then offered the packet to David. "So, what is it you think I hide from other people?"

"You're a thoroughly nice fellow," David began, "but you have an inner strength that you don't often let people see. I think it's a great surprise when others realise it is there, hovering just beyond the surface."

"Because I'm nice, people think I'm a soft touch?"

"Yes, that's just it."

"But if someone found that out about me, I'm not going to murder them just to keep that information quiet."

"Nooo," David extended the word as he blew out a stream of smoke. "But imagine if the Marquess blackmailed someone who he thinks, on the surface, has a mild personality like your own. Then he discovers a hidden layer. You'd do anything to protect Evelyn, wouldn't you?"

"You think the Marquess has tried to blackmail someone who has fought back?"

"Yes, I do." David nodded. "Everyone has their limits. A chap can only be pushed so far before he snaps."

Tommy considered his friend's words. "You have a very valid point. Unfortunately, I don't think that helps us at all."

"It doesn't?" David sounded disappointed. "I thought I'd given you the key to solve the murders."

"I'm afraid if silencing the Marquess's blackmail is the motive for his death, that doesn't rule anyone out."

"Perhaps if I can find out what it was about Sir Richard, that may help?"

"It may," Tommy said. "But really whatever the scandal was, it simply rules him in. There's nothing to rule anyone out."

"I think you and Evelyn need to go back to the beginning. Go through everything you know, and maybe then things will become clearer."

"You're right." Tommy tapped his cigar over the ashtray. "I think the biggest issue is we have so much information, and none of it makes any sense, but the answer is in there somewhere."

"I have every confidence in you, Northmoor." David sat back in his chair and grinned as though he'd solved the entire case himself.

He hadn't. But his friend had given him the belief in himself that he needed to go over the facts one more time with Evelyn and see if that helped them reach a conclusion.

# CHAPTER 12

*D*inner that evening was a very subdued event. After they had eaten, Detective Inspector Andrews announced that everyone was to meet in the billiard room. Helen, who had chosen to eat her meal in her bedroom, had shrieked at Montgomery that she refused to come downstairs. Eventually, however, everyone sat in the allotted room and an air of expectation crackled through the warm air.

"Why, yes," Tommy's voice could be heard clearly through the open doors to the terrace. "I know precisely who the murderer is."

"I did tell the detectives it wasn't me."

"Do not concern yourself, Harry. I think the detective arresting you for a crime you haven't committed must be some sort rite of passage a Christie man must endure. The very same thing happened to me."

"Alright, alright, Lord Northmoor!" Detective Inspector Andrews called. "We can hear you both very well. You can come back in now."

"Oh good," Aunt Em rubbed her hands together in glee. "I adore parlour games."

Evelyn moved to the front of the room and stood next to

144

the unlit fireplace. "That little charade was necessary to prove that voices carry from the terrace to the inside of this room, and vice versa."

"Wonderful." Les snapped. "Is that it? I'd like to pack my things tonight so I can get away from this place early tomorrow."

"I am very sorry your stay with us has been so very difficult for you, Mr Dawson," Evelyn said sympathetically.

"And now what is this you're doing?" he asked snidely. "Some sort of exhibition? Have I not suffered enough?"

"Do you want to know the identity of your wife's killer?" Tommy asked, moving to stand next to Evelyn.

Les stared pointedly at the police detectives standing near the closed inner door of the billiard room. "Isn't that their job?"

"Detective Inspector Andrews has kindly allowed us to speak," Evelyn said.

"I feel it prudent to point out that there are uniformed police officers stationed outside on the terrace." Tommy pointed through the doors. "So if someone felt inclined to make a run for it, they won't get very far. Now, shall we begin?"

"It will be no surprise to anyone present that the Marquess of York was not a popular man. We were soon to learn that he was a bully, incredibly unkind, and had a penchant for blackmail." Evelyn looked around the room. "That is to say, there were a number of people who would have been glad to see him dead."

Helen lit one of her cigarettes and dabbed at her eyes with a handkerchief. "That's an unpleasant thing to say about the dearly departed."

"It is," Evelyn agreed affably. "However, it's true."

"Andrew was a quite wonderful man," Helen said. "I think you're jealous. It's the only reason I can think of for you to talk such nonsense."

"I can assure you that is not the case," Evelyn said coolly.

"Mother," Tommy cut in. "I would advise you to think carefully about what you say next. Your words and decisions this weekend have already cost you dearly."

Helen's blue eyes glittered coldly. "What does that mean?"

"You chose to sell your home when you married the Marquess which, effectively, would leave your three younger children homeless. How do you think that made them feel?"

Helen effected a dramatic sob into her hankie. "The house will not now be sold. The girls and Harry can stay with me."

"We don't want to," Harry said clearly. "Not a single one of us. We shall stay here with Tommy and Evelyn where we have a secure home that is not dependent on a marriage of convenience."

"You would take children away from their own mother?" Helen turned her rage onto Evelyn, no trace of tears on her angry red face. "Is that because you can't have children of your own?"

"Mother!" Tommy stepped forward, stopping only when Evelyn put a hand on his arm. "I warned you about going too far."

"Everyone knows you've married a barren woman," Helen went on, completely unperturbed. "The entire village talks about how one sister has five healthy children, yet the other can't even manage one."

"How very sad they don't have something more interesting to talk about," Evelyn said softly. She refused to be brought down to Helen's level and start trading insults with her mother-in-law. It wouldn't do anyone any good. "Now, if we can move on."

"Why don't we stay with my mother?" Tommy suggested. "I know we were going to talk about her motives for killing Andrew last, but why don't you do it now?"

Evelyn heard the very slight emphasis Tommy placed on the word 'you'. They had agreed that he would handle their discussions into Helen's possible involvement in her fiancé's death, but by allowing her to do it, he was giving her the ammunition to fire some shots of her own back at his mother.

"What possible motive could I have for killing Andrew? I loved him."

"Your motive was obvious," Evelyn said. "He was a cruel man, and I think you knew that. Killing him was the only way you could escape a marriage that you realised would be quite dreadful."

"And why would I kill his daughter?"

"She heard you arguing with Andrew, and guessed that you had killed him. You were then forced to kill her to keep her quiet."

"I was in bed!" Helen said, outrage in her voice. "I couldn't have killed Beatrice."

"You could quite easily have got up, walked along the corridor, and pushed her out of the bedroom window. Unless you are now telling us that there was someone else in your bedroom who can vouch for you, you have no alibi for Beatrice's death."

"But I wouldn't—"

"Until this weekend I didn't think you would choose a man over your children, but you did." There was no hint of warmth in Tommy's voice and his gaze raked over his mother.

"The Marquess humiliated you by making you ask Tommy for a rather large sum of money," Evelyn went on.

"That was my idea," Helen said stubbornly. "Andrew would never make me do something I didn't want to do."

"Why did you ask for the money?"

"It was to be my dowry."

"I don't think I have ever heard of a middle-aged woman receiving a dowry from her son in polite society."

"I don't think I've ever heard of a woman entering a marriage with nothing but herself." Helen glanced around the room. "None of this belongs to you, it's all Tommy's. You were nothing before he married you."

"I believe you were the third daughter of a practically penniless vicar," Aunt Em's imperious voice sounded clearly throughout the room. "What was it you brought into your marriage with Henry?"

Helen looked down for a moment before regaining her composure. "I gave him four children. Without Tommy, we wouldn't all be sitting here now. Hessleham Hall would belong to some distant cousin."

"So, to recap." Evelyn paused deliberately. "You were taking a dowry into your marriage with the Marquess of York because he couldn't afford to support you without it?"

"I did not say that!" Helen screeched.

"Then what was it for?"

"Andrew said we would use the money for holidays as we aged."

"I thought you said asking Tommy for the money was your idea?"

"We decided together," Helen spat.

"Had you heard the same gossip I did about the Marquess and Lady Adeline Cameron?"

Helen flushed a mottled red and she sucked furiously on her cigarette holder. "I never listen to idle gossip."

"You see," Evelyn said in a deliberately conversational tone. "I think you were humiliated at asking your son for money. I also believe you were completely mortified when hearing that Andrew would have preferred a marriage to Lady Adeline so he had a chance for an heir, but she was as poor as him."

"That's just simply not true," Helen said stubbornly. "Andrew loved me."

"I believe the Marquess loved the idea of my husband's money, and nothing more."

"I did not kill him!"

"Oh, I see," Evelyn replied in a deliberately casual voice. "Then there must be an innocent explanation as to why one of your handkerchiefs was found covered in blood next to the Marquess's body?"

I...I don't—" Helen cast her eyes wildly around the room as though trying to find an explanation.

"Wait!" Detective Inspector Andrews said loudly, looking at Tommy. "What is this? Was there a piece of evidence you withheld?"

"Do forgive me, detective," Evelyn said. "This is completely my fault. I was so stunned to find the Marquess' body this morning, I picked up the handkerchief without thinking. I'm afraid to say that I then panicked and hid it, fearing my fingerprints would be on it, and I would be arrested. Just as you have arrested my poor husband and Harry in the past."

"We can't take fingerprints from a handkerchief, Lady Northmoor." The detective stared at Evelyn, looking very much like he wanted to put her into handcuffs and haul her off to York as punishment. "But I think you know that, don't you?"

"I'm very sorry," she said demurely.

"I also think you are aware that Harry wasn't arrested until after this event. What have you done with this crucial evidence?"

"I hid it."

"Really?" He raised an eyebrow but didn't look in the least bit shocked. "May I ask where?"

"Under a loose brick in the wall at the front of the chapel. Shall I show you?"

"That won't be necessary." He turned to Montgomery. "Send one of the chaps out to gather the evidence."

～

"*L*et's move along to discussing a different suspect," Tommy said without looking at his mother. He didn't need to. He could feel her eyes boring into him, but he steeled himself against the inevitable feelings of guilt her emotional upheaval caused him. What she had said to Evelyn was utterly unforgivable.

"I don't think you need to," Aunt Em said. "She seems guilty to me."

"That has been our problem all day," Tommy replied. "Every time we talk about our suspects, everyone seems guilty."

"I shall listen carefully." Em folded her hands in her lap. "But I shouldn't think you can convince me the murderer is anyone but that vindictive woman who purports to call herself your mother."

"We shall see." He smiled his thanks at his loyal great-aunt and turned to Frank Simmons. "Mr Simmons, let's talk about your relationship with the Marquess."

"I hated the man," Frank said honestly. "Absolutely and completely loathed him."

"But you were his best man," Helen said petulantly, as though she herself had been horribly let down by Frank.

"Doesn't mean I liked the fellow."

"You were blackmailed by him?" Tommy asked.

Frank stuck his pipe between his teeth, but did not light it. "I was."

"I do not intend to reveal the reason for that blackmail," Tommy said. "I have shared that information with the police, but it is not necessary everyone in the room hears the details."

Frank inclined his head slightly. "I'm grateful, Northmoor."

"Is that why we never have any money?" Jane asked in a high voice, bright pink spots on her cheeks. "Did you give that man our money for his silence?"

He met his wife's accusing glare without flinching. "I did, my love."

"What could he have possibly known about us that—" she broke off as, no doubt, the reason her husband was so keen to keep the Marquess quiet just occurred to her.

"Did you kill the Marquess?"

"I did not," Frank said. "But I cannot prove it."

"You were seen going towards the billiard room on the night he was killed. Did you argue with him that night?"

"I've never argued with the fellow in my life." Frank took his pipe out of his mouth and struck a match. "I valued our family secrets too much."

"And now that he is dead, your life will be much easier will it not?"

"Very much so." Frank puffed contentedly on his pipe. "I would go so far as to say I would jolly well like to shake the hand of the person who killed the Marquess."

"Can you tell me where you were when Lady Beatrice was killed?"

"I was in my room."

"You were not," Tommy said with certainty.

"Now, see here, Northmoor. I have been very honest with you."

"Perhaps you have," Tommy agreed. "But on this occasion, you are being decidedly untruthful. Unless, of course, you are to admit to killing Lady Beatrice?"

"I would never do such a thing. Lady Beatrice was a nice lady. She didn't deserve to die for her father's sins."

"We don't believe she died because of anything her father did. It is more likely that she heard someone arguing with her father that night, and she was killed to prevent her from telling the police who that person was."

"I didn't argue with him," Frank said, this time a little more forcefully. "And I was in my room when Lady Beatrice died."

"Then perhaps you can tell us who killed her?"

"Me?" Frank jabbed a thumb toward his own chest. "Why would I know? I keep telling you. I have nothing to do with this whole dirty business."

"Lady Beatrice fell from the window in your room."

Frank looked at Jane, then back to Tommy. "That can't be."

"We have verified that your bedroom is the only one that could have caused Lady Beatrice's body to fall where it did." Detective Inspector Andrews looked gravely at Frances Lester. "And, besides, Lady Frances saw her sister standing in that very room before she was pushed out."

"Would you like to change your story?"

"I didn't kill her," Frank said stubbornly.

❦

"Shall we move along?" Evelyn suggested. "Mrs Simmons?"

"Me?" Jane squeaked.

"You told me how unkind the Marquess was to your husband and how he took every single opportunity to make the both of you feel inferior to him. You also spoke in detail about how much you admired his wife, Clara."

"That old frump?" Helen snapped. "Andrew said she couldn't even be bothered to get up from her bed when guests came to the house. How excruciatingly embarrassing that was for him. A Marchioness should always be willing to support her husband in every way possible."

Helen sounded as though she was reading from a pamphlet Andrew had written and given to her detailing the correct behaviour for a woman of a certain class.

"Did he also tell you that was because she couldn't?" Jane's usually mild expression had turned to a twisted mask of fury. "The poor darling couldn't get out of bed because he caused a horse-riding accident that paralysed her."

"You vicious cat!" Helen screamed. "Andrew would never do such a thing."

"Actually," Frances said in a tired voice. "That sounds exactly like the sort of thing Father would do if it suited his purposes."

"You didn't know him like I did." Helen pouted.

"Mrs Christie," Frances said with exaggerated patience. "You knew him precisely two minutes. I have known the man my entire life. He was a tyrant."

"Perhaps if you had tried being less of a—"

"Stop!" Tommy said loudly, his gaze on Helen. "I will not have you insulting our guests."

"They're not your guests."

"They may be here at your invitation, but they are in my house. Now, either be quiet until we have unravelled this whole sorry mess, or I shall have you removed from my home."

Helen opened her mouth to argue, seemed to realise what a terrible idea that was, then stared mutinously back at Evelyn.

"Did the Marquess' cruelty towards his wife, and his arrogance when dealing with your husband lead you to kill him?"

"Like my husband, I should like to give my thanks to the person who did it."

"And where were you when Lady Beatrice died? You were asked to join Lady Frances, Lady Emily, and me out on the terrace for afternoon tea but you declined. What did you do instead?"

"I was reading in the library. As you know, I had started a new book. I was completely engrossed and didn't want to put it down for a moment."

"What is it about?"

"It's a murder mystery," Jane said cautiously, clearly realising that Evelyn's questions were designed to catch her out.

"Who are the main characters?"

"The detective." Jane's face flushed again. "And the other fellow, I don't remember his name. I'm afraid I'm not good with names, Lady Northmoor."

"What do you remember about the book I read to Lady Emily before dinner?"

"Oh!" Jane's face lit up. "That was about a horse, Black Beauty. Such a wonderful book."

"What was the young girl called?"

"Jo," Jane responded, her face showing confusion.

"But you don't remember anything about the book that caught your attention earlier today?"

"No."

"Mrs Simmons, were you in fact reading a book in the library or were you upstairs preparing to shove poor Lady Beatrice from your bedroom window?"

"I can't read!" Jane blurted out, then looked down at her hands. "That is, I can, but very slowly."

"You didn't leave the library?"

"I did not," Jane confirmed. "But I don't have anyone who can verify that. I was alone."

"Do you know why your husband would claim to be in your room when there was no way he could have been. Unless, of course, he was the murderer?"

"The only reason Frank would ever lie is to protect me." She looked at her husband and smiled. "Of that I am certain."

"Thank you, Mrs Simmons." Evelyn looked at Tommy. "Shall we move on, darling?"

# CHAPTER 13

"Sir Richard," Tommy said. "If we may move on to you?"

"Of course, my boy," Sir Richard smiled genially. "But, as I have already told you, I barely knew the Marquess."

"You told Evelyn you may have deep secrets."

He turned to Evelyn and let out a deep laugh. "That was just a silly jape. You must surely both know that."

"This is a murder investigation." Tommy indicated the police detectives standing on the other side of the fireplace. "You must know that telling the truth is extremely important."

"I would never lie to the police," he said.

"Should I get Detective Inspector Andrews to ask you the next question?" Tommy disliked what he was about to do, but he didn't have a choice. "As you have insinuated you wouldn't tell me the truth."

"I respect law and order in this country."

"I've spoken to colleagues at Scotland Yard who would suggest that is not strictly true," Detective Inspector Andrews retorted. "I do not intend to speak about the nature of the crime in front of everyone, but I am certain you know what I am referring to."

"I can assure you I do not," Sir Richard said in a haughty voice.

The detective drew an envelope from the inside pocket of his jacket and took out a sheet of paper. "On the third day of March nineteen twenty-two, you were apprehended inside—"

"Enough!" Sir Richard's voice boomed throughout the large room.

"Did the Marquess somehow have knowledge of this event and use it to blackmail you?" Tommy asked gently.

"Yes." Sir Richard covered his face with his hands. "I paid a tidy sum to keep the matter hush-hush, but obviously someone blabbed."

"What happened with the Marquess?"

"He asked to speak to me privately after dinner. He suggested I could pay him a sum of money to keep his mouth shut."

"And did you agree to that? Or did you arrange to meet him later that night and kill him?"

"I agreed to his terms," Sir Richard said insistently, "and promised to give him a cheque the next day."

"Did you know your argument was overheard?"

"I had no idea," he admitted. "But that doesn't change my answer. I did not kill the Marquess and I certainly did not kill his poor daughter."

"You were here in the billiard room when Lady Beatrice was killed?"

"That is correct." Sir Richard ducked his head. "As I explained, I had fallen asleep. Unfortunately that happens quite often at my age. The first I knew anything was amiss was when I heard Lady Frances screaming."

"How did you feel about my mother marrying the Marquess?"

"He didn't seem like the most pleasant of fellows, but Helen was rather excited about the whole thing. As her godfather, I was only too happy to step in and give her away."

"Were you not concerned he might be abusive towards her?"

"I do not think you give your mother enough credit, Thomas." Sir Richard's tone had turned sharp. "She can take care of herself."

That was in direct opposition to what he had said earlier when he suggested Harry needed to take better care of his mother. However, Tommy's idea that perhaps Sir Richard could be romantically interested in his mother couldn't have been more wrong. He had learned that the man was capable of saying something and then almost believe its veracity himself.

~

"*L*ady Frances, may we talk to you next?"

Frances Lester lifted a shoulder in resignation. "If you must."

"Your father was very scathing in his remarks towards you and your sister the night he died."

"Neither of us particularly noticed," Frances replied. "Father was no different last night than he was any other night. It pains me to say, but we had both become rather accustomed to his insults."

"Do you wish you had stood up to him?"

"I wish we could have."

"You don't think there was something you could've done to change the way he behaved?"

"No, I do not." Tears filled Frances' eyes and she fished in her handbag. Pulling out a well-used handkerchief, she dabbed at her eyes. "The only thing I wish I'd done is kill

Father myself. If I'd done that, the murderer would not have needed to silence Beatrice and she would still be here with us. My heart breaks every time I think of her poor children."

"You don't see any other motive for Beatrice being killed other than to keep her quiet?"

"She told me herself she had overheard an argument between Father and someone else. I wish I had pressed her into telling me who it was. I wish I had begged her to take care of herself and not go anywhere alone until the fiend was caught." Frances looked at Evelyn beseechingly. "Please tell me you know the identity of the murderer."

"We believe so," Evelyn confirmed. "Have you had an opportunity to discuss your husband's identity with him?"

"Yes, but Nicholas's true identity does not have anything to do with either Father's or Beatrice's murders."

"How can you be so sure?"

"No one knew who he was until you worked it out."

"That's not strictly true," Evelyn said gently. "Nicholas knew who he was and what your father's death would mean for him."

"Taxes and poverty," Nicholas snapped. "Certainly nothing worth killing a man for."

"What is this?" Les frowned. "What are you all talking about?"

"Nicholas's full name is Nicholas Lester Parsons. He's Reginald's son."

"Reginald?" Les repeated, his face clouded with confusion.

"Father's youngest brother."

"Are you saying Nicholas is your father's heir?"

"It appears so," Frances said in a tired voice.

Les jumped to his feet. "You killed Beatrice!"

Nicholas held his hands out in front of his body to ward off Les. "I didn't kill anyone. Les, we're friends. You know I would never do something like that."

"You could've killed the old man," Les retorted. "God knows we've talked about it enough."

"Les—"

"What?" He took another step towards Nicholas. "Stop talking about the amount of times we've said we wished we were brave enough to take out the man who made all of our lives a misery."

"I know you're angry and grieving, but I don't think this is the right time—" Nicholas looked pointedly around the room, his gaze stopping on the detectives, "—or place to discuss this."

"Oh, I think I'd like to hear what Mr Dawson has to say," Detective Inspector Andrews said. "Mr Dawson, if you could explain?"

Les finally seemed to understand the potential implications of what he was saying. "Silly things we said to one another when we'd had a few too many after dinner brandies."

"You joked about killing my father?"

"Don't sit there all innocent and virtuous, Frances," Les said roughly. "Not when I know you had similar conversations with Beatrice."

"She told you?"

"We told each other everything." Les put a hand over his eyes. "But now all that is gone. My darling wife is gone."

"Where were you when your wife was killed?" Evelyn asked.

Les looked up at Evelyn, tears running down his face. "I have told you. I was in the garden."

"You did tell me that," Evelyn agreed. "However, you forget that I was present when your wife was pushed from the upstairs window. You arrived on the scene from the direction of the house."

"I came in through the front door." Les pointed wildly. "From the direction of the garden."

"You did not," Evelyn contradicted. "I have already checked that with Malton. He was standing in the corridor outside the billiard room. No one entered the house from the front door, or the small side entrance near the office the detectives have been using."

"Mr Lester?" Evelyn raised an eyebrow. "Or should we use your title?"

"If you were a real lady," Helen said. "You would know that an heir does not use his title until after the funeral of the person whose title he is to inherit."

"It takes a lot more than a fancy title to be a real lady," Evelyn retorted. "But I shouldn't suppose you would know that because you have no experience of either."

Helen crushed the cigarette she had been smoking into an ashtray. She muttered something, but Evelyn was too far away to hear her words clearly.

"As you've just proved Les here wasn't in the garden, there is no point in me claiming I was there too, is there?"

"Not really," Evelyn said quietly. "Do either of you want to explain where you were?"

"We were together," Nicholas said. "Talking about what would happen to us, to our home, following the Marquess' death."

"And never once did you tell me you were his heir!" Les exclaimed bitterly. "Not once did you even intimate you knew who it was. Even though we discussed that very subject at great length."

"I'm sorry, old man," Nicholas said. "I should've. The truth is, I still don't know if I will even petition the Lord Chancellor for a writ of summons for the title. I'm not sure I can see the point."

"I think you must," Les said. "Maybe something good can come out of what has happened?"

Nicholas laughed bitterly. "All I see are death duties that I have no hope of meeting."

"Perhaps you should make a decision when you know the full scale of your liabilities? Perhaps there will be a trust that gives you an annual income? There usually is in these situations."

"Why are you so keen?" Nicholas said, his eyes narrowing as he looked at Les. "Oh, of course, I see—George!"

George was Les and Beatrice's son and therefore Nicholas's nephew. Did that make him Nicholas's heir, should he prove his identity and take on the title of Marquess of York? Evelyn wasn't sure. She was certain Helen would know, but it wasn't her concern and she didn't think it had any implications on the investigation.

She did hope that the fractured Parsons/Lester/Dawson family would put aside their differences and find a way to forge a strong union together. After all, Les had given Nicholas a job when he needed one and they were family. Family, in her opinion, were almost always stronger together than when divided.

~

"Now we have spoken to everyone, I hope you can see how very difficult it was for us," Tommy said. "Each person has a reason or, as the police would call it, a motive to kill the Marquess of York. Secondary to that was the death of Lady Beatrice. She was killed so she could not reveal the name of the person she heard arguing with her father."

"But how did the killer know Beatrice had overheard that argument?" Harry asked.

"A very good question," Tommy answered. "And it's the reason I had you come outside and have that little conversation with me earlier."

"We could hear every word," Evelyn said.

"And so, earlier today, I spoke to Constance who had also been in the billiard room last night. I wondered if she had seen anyone going in, or out, of that room. I mentioned that Lady Beatrice had overheard an argument."

"And you think the killer was listening outside?" Harry asked doubtfully.

"Maybe he was listening on purpose hoping to hear something useful. Maybe he was simply outside and happened to hear what we were discussing and realised he could use it to his advantage."

"I still think he should've just admitted to arguing with the Marquess," Aunt Em said. "There was no need for Lady Beatrice to die."

"I'm afraid the killer didn't think like that. When he realised there was one more person who knew his secret, and could reveal it to the world at any time, he decided Lady Beatrice must be silenced too."

"Mother?" Tommy turned to Helen.

"This is getting ridiculous." She shook her head, anger radiating from her.

"Who did you give your missing handkerchief to?"

Helen's eyes darted to Sir Richard, before landing back on Tommy. "I don't know what you mean."

"You had six in a set. One was in your handbag, there were four left in the drawer. What happened to the other?"

"Anyone could've gone into my room and taken it." Helen raised her hands, palms up. "I don't know why you are making such a drama out of it."

"It was found next to the dead body of your fiancé," Tommy said. "Either you're covering for someone, or you are protecting yourself."

Helen pursed her lips, and Tommy turned away from her, disgust at her behaviour roiling in his stomach.

"Sir Richard?"

"I have no need for a woman's handkerchief, my boy, I have my own."

"Mother gave it to you, didn't she? You were to give her

away. Did she give it to you in case she needed it during the ceremony? She certainly had nowhere to keep a hankie, did she?"

"I don't know why you are attacking your mother and me, Tommy, but it must stop."

"I'm not attacking you, Sir Richard," Tommy said, sadness crushing his chest. "I am unveiling a murderer."

"Why would I kill the Marquess?"

"We have already gone over that," Tommy replied. "I got so far, and then you begged me to say no more."

"I paid the man," Sir Richard barked.

"Did you agree too easily so he then got greedy and asked for more? Is that why you stabbed him?"

"I didn't think I would ever be ashamed to know you, Thomas Christie, but I am."

"Maybe you can explain something to me?" Evelyn asked.

"What do you want to know?" he asked wearily.

"If you were sitting right about where you are now," she said questioningly. "Why did it take you so long to get out onto the terrace?"

He hesitated, only momentarily, but it was long enough to convince Tommy they were on the right track. "I told you, I was asleep. It took a few moments for me to understand what was happening. You must understand what I am, Lady Emily?"

Sir Richard smiled at Lady Emily who gazed coolly back at him. "I do not take afternoon naps. And, if I did, I would awake with all my faculties in good working order. It would not take me as long as you did to walk the short distance from this room to the terrace, and I am a great deal older than you."

"This is ridiculous." Sir Richard threw up his hands. "You can't attempt to convict me based on how long it takes me to walk from one place to another."

"It's not our job to convict you, Sir Richard." Tommy

nodded toward Detective Inspector Andrews. "It is the police's. If you are telling the truth, I assume the cheque you wrote to the Marquess will be either on his person or amongst the possessions in his room. Has anything like that been found?"

"It has not, My Lord."

"It seems to me that taking one's cheque book to dinner is a very odd practice."

"It's quite usual for me," Sir Richard said. "It's habit. I take it everywhere with me in London."

"So your bank will have a record of all the places you have used cheques?"

"I would imagine so." Perspiration stood out on the older man's forehead.

"Montgomery, telephone to Scotland Yard. Give them instructions to obtain records from Sir Richard's bank first thing in the morning."

"Yes, sir." Montgomery stood to leave the room.

"Wait a moment," Tommy said. "Perhaps it would be wise to get some witness accounts at some of Sir Richard's gentleman's clubs? Maybe he paid cash in some establishments and someone would be willing to say he was seen in there?"

"Please don't say anymore, my boy." Sir Richard shook his head sadly, as a bead of sweat rolled down the side of his face. "I cannot stand anymore."

"I am not your boy," Tommy said sharply. "I have never been your boy. How could you do it?"

"My reputation is everything to me," Sir Richard mumbled. "I couldn't have that man besmirching my good name."

"How did he know?"

Sir Richard pulled at his collar with one finger. "He had a friend who had heard a rumour. I could have denied it. But it seemed easier to just pay him. He was marrying Helen the very next day. I hoped I could use my influence to persuade the Marquess to find someone else to blackmail. Because I never had a moment's doubt that the payment he demanded last night would be the only one."

"You took the cheque back when you killed him?"

"Yes, I got blood on my hands. Used Helen's handkerchief to wipe my hands clean."

"And what of Lady Beatrice?"

Sir Richard looked at Les. "You must believe me, Mr Dawson, I didn't want that to happen. But she knew, you see. I had to keep her quiet."

"How did you lure her into the Simmonses' room?"

"I heard her say she was going for a lie down, followed her upstairs, and pushed her into the nearest bedroom." He looked down at his hands, and this time when moisture fell down his face, Tommy could see that it was tears. "She was very afraid. I told her I wasn't going to hurt her I just wanted her assurance that she wasn't going to reveal my secret."

"I can't believe she would've told the police about you," Les said. "We all detested him."

"She didn't mention to us that she had overheard anyone arguing with her father," the detective confirmed.

"I pretended to have some problems breathing and she calmed down, then opened the window for me. When she turned back around, I shoved her as hard as I could. She stumbled backward, and the rest you know."

"You killed two people to prevent your secrets from being made public," Nicholas said, staring at Sir Richard in disgust. "How could you?"

Sir Richard got to his feet. "You are going to arrest me, now?"

"Yes," Detective Inspector Andrews said.

"May I ask for one courtesy?"

"Did you afford my sister such niceties?" Frances said, her voice sad and very quiet.

"I did not, Lady Frances, and it is to my eternal shame."

"What do you want?" Tommy asked roughly.

"Simply to take off my dinner suit, and travel to York in my comfortable clothes."

"Comfortable clothes?" Les shrieked. "You vile human being!"

"Let's get him out of here," Detective Inspector Andrews said to his colleague. "Northmoor?"

Tommy looked at Sir Richard for a long moment, and then nodded. "Allowing him to change won't hurt."

# CHAPTER 14

"*D*id you know he was going to do that?" Aunt Em asked later that evening as the family sat together in the drawing room.

"I had my suspicions."

"Do you think that was justice for that poor family?" Evelyn asked angrily. "You should have let the police take him away instead of allowing him to decide his own fate. Who are you to decide what punishment a murderer should have?"

"He will receive a judgement from someone far mightier than I."

"Perhaps," Aunt Em agreed. "But Evelyn is right. You have denied Lady Beatrice's family justice here on earth by giving Sir Richard the chance to shoot himself."

"I thought he deserved a little dignity."

"He didn't allow Lady Beatrice any, did he?" Evelyn got to her feet. "I am disappointed in you, Tommy."

He watched his wife flee from the room as sadness over-whelmed him.

"You can't blame her anger, Tommy," Aunt Em said. "She found a body this morning, and then witnessed a murder. On top of that, she has had to listen to your mother's vile insults. You must do something to regain her trust and admiration."

He pulled a hand through his hair and gestured towards the door. "She clearly cannot stand to even be in the same room as me at the moment."

"Yes," Aunt Em said. "We all noticed that. I fear this time, you must do something spectacular. Simply allowing your wife to have another dog is not going to win her around."

"I don't—"

"She has given up her entire way of life to be your wife," Aunt Em went on, her voice low but all the more powerful because of her delivery. "With no training, or preparation, she has stepped into becoming a quite wonderful Countess of Northmoor. I don't think the girl has any idea of her worth to both you, the estate, and the family in general."

"I am worried that Evelyn feels her worth to me is tied up with her ability to give me a child."

Aunt Em pointed at Tommy. "Then it is up to you to convince your wife she is wrong."

"I—"

"Now," Aunt Em said with steely determination. "I have been promised a celebration and I refuse to participate until you have made your peace with Evelyn."

Tommy hurried up to their bedroom. Doris jumped as he roughly pushed open the door. "Oh, Lord Northmoor, you gave me a fright!"

"I'm terribly sorry, Doris. I was looking for Lady Northmoor."

"I thought she was downstairs with you." Doris got to her feet. "I shall look for her."

"No no." Tommy waved a hand. "It has to be me that finds her."

He patted the dogs as he left the room. Where would she have fled to? Almost as soon as he asked himself the question, he knew. She would be in the kitchen, visiting her friends.

As he descended the kitchen stairs, he heard feminine laughter. "Oh, Lady Northmoor, you didn't!"

Tommy felt guilty standing next to the door, eavesdropping on his wife, and not attempting to make himself known.

"I certainly did," Evelyn said. "Now, where is Nora?"

A chair scraped across the kitchen floor and Tommy stepped into the doorway before he was discovered. "Good evening, Cook."

"Oh, Lord Northmoor!" Mrs O'Connell hastily got to her feet.

"Please," he said. "Sit down, relax. I haven't come down here to check up on you, only to find my wife."

"I came downstairs to tell Nora about the arrangements we have made," Evelyn said stiffly. "Where did you say she was, Cook?"

"I didn't," Mrs O'Connell mumbled.

"Do you know where she is?"

"She may be outside."

"May be?"

"Albert sometimes comes up to the house on an evening." Mrs O'Connell flushed. "Just to say goodnight, like."

"I shall fetch them." Tommy strode to the back door.

Nora and Albert jumped apart and stared in horror at Tommy. Evelyn followed behind him. "You've scared them both half to death, Tommy! Nora, Albert, come inside. We have something to tell you."

Warily the young couple followed Tommy and Evelyn back into the kitchen. Tommy was aware of Mrs O'Connell performing some sort of wild hand gestures in Nora's direction, but he ignored her. "Lady Northmoor has something exciting she would like to share with you."

"Now," Evelyn started, smiling at each of them in turn. "You don't have to say yes. We have arranged all of this behind your backs, I am afraid, which is a little naughty of us. I got rather carried away with the excitement of Miss

Madeleine marrying Mr Ryder and thought how splendid it would be to take advantage of the wonderful feast you have all worked so hard to make for our family."

"Evelyn." Tommy nudged his wife. "Get to the point."

"Lord Northmoor and Lord Chesden have arranged a Special Licence for Miss Madeleine and Mr Ryder to marry tomorrow morning."

"A wedding on a Monday morning?" Nora frowned. "Isn't that a strange day on which to get married?"

"It is rather unusual," Evelyn agreed. "The exciting thing is, we have also got a Special Licence for you and Albert."

Nora sucked in a shocked breath and covered her mouth with her hands. "You didn't!"

"We most certainly did."

"Partridge has been busy today getting one of the cottages ready for you," Tommy added. "It might not be as clean as you would like it, but it's yours."

"Lord Northmoor." Albert extended a hand to Tommy. "I don't know how to thank you, sir."

"My Lord," Mrs O'Connell hissed.

"Lord Northmoor, My Lord," Albert said. "Thank you from the very bottom of my heart. I promise I will take care of Nora to the very best of my ability until my dying day."

"Oh my goodness, lad!" Cook exclaimed. "He's her employer, not her father!"

"I know you're going to tell me off." Nora shot a glance towards the cook. "But I don't care!"

The young girl threw her arms around Evelyn. "I don't think I will ever be as happy as I am right in this moment. When I came here from the orphanage, I didn't think for a minute I would know a lady as grand as you. You have made all of my dreams come true."

"Oh, get on with you," Cook muttered as she lifted the corner of her apron to dab at her eyes.

"If you are truly happy," Evelyn said, as she returned

Nora's embrace, "then the powers of persuasion I used on my husband were worth it."

She smiled at Tommy over the top of Nora's head. He wanted to pull her into his own arms and tell her how proud he was of her, but a sense of propriety stopped him. Then he remembered Aunt Em's words.

As Nora stepped back to stand next to Albert, Tommy caught hold of Evelyn's hand and dropped to one knee in front of her.

"Tommy, what are you doing?" She glanced nervously around at the others.

"My darling," he said. "I want you to know how very honoured I am to be your husband. If it were possible to marry you again, I would do it every single day for the rest of my life."

Albert nodded in admiration, cook sniffed, and Nora grinned broadly.

"Tommy, do get up." She tugged on his hand as her cheeks pinkened.

"I haven't finished," he told her. "I don't always get things right, and for that I'm sorry. Being with you makes me a better man. I am proud of everything that you do for other people, but most of all I am proud that you chose me as your husband."

"Now have you finished?" she whispered as she wiped her eyes.

"Yes," he said. "I think so. At least, I have finished if I am forgiven. Am I?"

"I shall think about it," Evelyn offered her cheek to Tommy and he leaned forward to press his lips quickly on her soft skin.

*T*he following day was every bit as hot as the previous week. However, no one allowed the heat to stop the preparations. Some of the flowers had wilted in the chapel, but they were quickly replaced by the village florist.

Madeleine had borrowed Evelyn's own wedding dress. Nora refused to wear anything that she termed 'grand' but had agreed to wear a simple white, drop-waisted dress that Evelyn had once worn when she attended Wimbledon. David and Albert wore their best suits.

John Capes, the vicar, hurried between the house and the chapel to make sure everything was ready for what would be a joint wedding.

"It's jolly unconventional," he commented to Tommy in a quiet moment.

"Madeleine and David are happy with the arrangements. Nora and Albert are over the moon they are able to marry sooner than they hoped." Tommy shrugged. "If everyone is happy, who cares about convention?"

"And Evelyn?"

"She has been up since before dawn organising dresses, hats, and whatever else it is women like to have for weddings."

"Your mother?"

"Partridge took her back to her house in the village an hour ago." Tommy frowned. "I don't know when I will next see her. She owes Evelyn an apology."

"From what I have seen, that may be some time in coming."

"I expect we shall next hear from Mother when she wants something from us," Tommy said sourly.

"Have your other guests left?"

"Everyone except Frank and Jane Simmons. They are staying for a few days. He's a rather nice chap. Of course,

Lord Chesden has stayed on for his brother's wedding, he is to be the best man."

"What on earth?" John turned around as a heavily perspiring Harry pushed the piano out of the library and into the hallway.

"Harry?"

"There isn't an organ in the chapel," Harry said, as if that were explanation enough.

"You surely don't mean to wheel the piano all the way to the chapel?"

Harry shrugged. "Can't think of any other way to get it there, and the girls insist they must have one."

"I think the easiest way is through the billiard room, out through the doors, and across the lawn." Tommy shook his head at the vicar. "Do excuse me vicar, I think my brother needs my help."

"One more thing," John said. "Does Albert have a best man?"

Tommy felt his face heat. "He's actually asked me to stand with him."

John shook his head and chuckled. "Just when I think things in this house can't get any more extraordinary, I realise I can still be shocked."

Tommy moved next to Harry and, together, they pushed the piano down the hallway.

"Tommy! What are you doing?" Evelyn called.

He turned to her, a smile on his face. "Harry tells me the girls insist on a piano in the chapel."

She kissed his cheek. "That's a splendid idea. Do carry on. Malton, how much more time do we have before the weddings?"

"Forty-five minutes, My Lady."

"Marvellous, I have just enough time for a large gin and tonic before I get myself ready for the wedding."

173

"Lady Emily is already in the drawing room enjoying a drink."

Evelyn hurried into the room and sat next to Aunt Em. "Is everything alright, dear?"

She kissed Em's cheek. "Things couldn't be any better. Tommy and Harry are taking the piano out to the chapel, Madeleine and Nora are to marry the men they love, and the sun is shining on us."

"The sun shone on this family when you and Tommy inherited this house." Aunt Em's eyes filled with tears. "Now it is full of family, which is exactly how it should be."

"Aunt Em," Evelyn leaned forward. "Are you crying?"

"Don't be ridiculous, dear." Aunt Em gestured to the sun streaming in through the tall windows. "The sun is in my eyes."

\*\*\*

Murder at Rochester Park, Book 6 in the Tommy & Evelyn mystery series is now available for pre-order.

# A NOTE FROM CATHERINE

Thank you very much for reading *Murder at the Wedding Chapel*! I had so much fun writing this story and I very much hope you enjoyed reading it. If you did, please consider leaving a review. Not only do reviews help other readers decide if *Murder at the Wedding Chapel* is something they might like to read but they also help me know what readers did, and did not enjoy, about my book.

If you would like to be amongst the first to know about my new releases, why not join my monthly newsletter. You can find the link on my website: www.catherinecoles.com

I also have Facebook group for fans of cozy mysteries. It's a place where we can chat about the books we've read, the things we like about cozies, any TV programmes in the cozy genre etc.. It is also the place where I will be sharing what I'm writing, price drops and also letting readers know about any FREE ARCs that may be available. More details can be found on my website.

Warmest wishes,

Catherine

9 781915 126047